KHOL
RESCUED BY THE ALIEN

BRIDES OF THE ZULDRUX WARRIORS

AVA ROSS

ENCHANTED STAR PRESS

Khol

Rescued by the Alien Series

Also part of the Brides of the Zuldrux Warriors Series

Copyright © 2024 Ava Ross

All rights reserved.

Cover Art: Natasha Snow Designs

Editing: JA Wren and Owl Eyes Proofs & Edits

*For my readers.
I couldn't do this without you!*

Also by Ava Ross

You can find Ava's books on Amazon

& on her website

KHOL

Can a single mom survive and find love in a new and exciting alien world?

Nancy: One moment, I'm a single mom picking up my four-year-old daughter from daycare, the next, we're shooting toward an alien planet in a space pod, crashing far from Earth. So much for giving my little girl the Christmas she's been dreaming of. At this rate, we'll be lucky to survive the next twenty-four hours.

Then a big, blue-skinned alien scoops us up in his arms and takes us to a lush, tropical paradise where he settles us into his home. If I didn't keep catching him gazing at me with longing, I'd think this stoic guy was a confirmed loner. When he helps us bring Christmas to this strange new world, all to please me and my daughter, I begin to wonder if life here might not be so bad after all. But I was burned in the past. Do I dare trust my heart to someone new?

Khol: My clan didn't need to banish me. I did it myself, settling on an uninhabited island where I resigned myself to being alone for the rest of my days. But then a ship crashes near my home. I rush there to salvage what I can, only to rescue a woman and her child. As I help them settle into my home, I start wondering if a male such as me is deserving of a life full of love.

I'm falling for Nancy, but I must atone for my past. If I give her and her daughter the holiday they crave, will I be worthy of a new chance at joy?

Khol is part of the Rescued by the Alien shared world and the Brides of the Zuldrux Warriors Series, and is a cozy/steamy romance with a lonely but determined hero and a woman who hopes to build a new, better life for herself and her young daughter. Expect heat, heart, and holiday fun.

Brides of the Zuldrux Warriors in order:
Craved by the Alien Beast
Treasured by the Alien Rogue
Claimed by the Alien Barbarian
Khol (part of the Rescued by the Alien Holiday Series)
Cherished by the Alien Outlaw
Adored by the Alien Warlord

CHAPTER 1
NANCY

"Time to go home, sweetie," I told my four-year-old daughter, Flora, smiling as she left her daycare friends and rushed toward me, the skirt of her bright pink dress fluffing around her knees. My daughter saw herself as a princess, as she should.

I couldn't love her more. So what if her dad bailed on us the moment I told him I was pregnant? I was determined right then to give my child all the love she needed.

As for my heart? I wasn't sure I'd ever trust it to someone new.

Flora wrapped her arms around my legs and grinned up at me. "Santa. Santa's coming soon!"

"Yes, Santa comes in a few days." I'd hidden her stuffed stocking and the few gifts I could afford in my closet, and after we'd set out cookies and milk for Santa and she'd fallen asleep, I'd place her gifts beneath the tree and drape her stocking across the back of the sofa.

I hadn't been able to buy much. Working two jobs paid our rent and her daycare, plus put food on the table, but there was rarely much left for extras. Still, she was young enough to enjoy opening her presents, and I was sure she'd adore the doll I'd scrimped on my own meals to save enough to buy for her. "Are you ready to go home?"

"Yes," she declared, flashing her baby teeth my way once more.

I stroked her rich brown hair from her face and pulled an elastic band from my pocket, making a quickie ponytail at the top of her head. The up-do I'd arranged for her this morning had come undone.

"Grab your bag from your cubby," I said, smiling at Janet, the woman who ran this daycare. It might not be fancy, but Janet kept her home clean, and it was clear she loved each child as if they were her own.

"She's such a good girl," Janet said, coming over to stand with me while Flora tugged her child-sized bright pink backpack from the wooden cubby mounted on the wall in the entryway. "I hope you two have an amazing Christmas."

It was Friday, and we'd celebrate Christmas eve on Monday. Fortunately, a single woman had offered to cover my shift on Tuesday so I could spend the day with Flora. My elderly neighbor would watch Flora on Monday while I worked, since Janet's daycare was closed.

"You too." I gave her a quick hug, and she patted my back.

"I'll see you on Wednesday?" Janet asked Flora, stroking her shoulder.

"Yes!" Flora chirped, hopping around with her bag in hand.

"Come on, sweetie," I said, taking her other hand. We stepped outside the tiny house while Janet hurried back to supervise the rest of the kids.

We'd started down the front walk when a robocop S.W.A.T. vehicle pulled into Janet's driveway. Frowning, I stopped and tucked my daughter behind me. Were they making a raid somewhere close?

Not long ago, AI robocops were introduced by a billionaire entrepreneur, and in no time, they'd taken over all the major city's police protection units. Though horribly expensive, they quickly proved they were worth the cost. Robocops didn't complain, they worked all hours, and they rarely broke down. Now that they patrolled the streets, crime was pretty much nonexistent. Who'd break the law when a robot would come after you? They could outrun, outthink, and outsmart the person before they could finish committing the crime.

Flora peeked around my legs as three robocops stormed out of the vehicle. Instead of racing across the road or wherever they'd been programmed to attack, they stomped toward me.

I backed toward Janet's front porch. Should we hide in the bushes flanking the side of the steps? I didn't want to get in their way.

The lead robocop's eyes flared, and a bright red dot appeared on the front of my shirt.

With a yelp, I swept Flora up in my arms and raced along the walk leading around the back of Janet's house. The robocops came after me, their metal footsteps clanging on the pavement at a pace much too rapid for me to outrun.

"I didn't do anything," I cried out as they grabbed my arm, nearly wrenching it from the socket. It was all I could do to hold onto Flora.

When they tried to pluck her from my arms, I bellowed and clung to her, falling to my knees. Flora wailed, and I tumbled forward, landing hard on my side, curling around her, holding tight.

One of the cops stabbed my precious daughter with a needle while another poked me in the upper arm.

The world swirled away and . . .

"Wake," a lilting voice said. "It's time for you to meet your fated mate."

My eyes popped open, and I tried to orient myself. Flora was nestled in my arms, and we lay inside a glass case. Frowning, I stared through the clear panel a few inches above our bodies, trying to figure out why we appeared to be riding in a narrow pod with stars whirling around us.

A blink told me this wasn't a dream.

Memories rushed through me of robocops taking us somewhere in a van, how one of them held us as it leaped over a very tall fence topped with wire that zapped and hummed. How the robocop placed me and Flora inside a . . .

A space pod much like this one.

Fear jolted through me, and I wanted to cry out, but more than that, I didn't want to scare my daughter. I bit down on my lips, compressing them together to hold back my wail.

A fierce need to keep my little girl safe shot through me, and I stilled my shakes.

Flora continued to slumber in my arms, and her soft breathing reassured me. I'd figure this out. We were going to be alright.

Where were we?

Lights blasted around the tip of the pod by my feet as we entered the outer atmosphere of an unknown planet. I'd studied astronomy in high school, and I'd enjoyed learning about the planets within our galaxy. The one the pod was approaching at a dizzying speed didn't look like anything from my textbook.

Flora stirred before falling back asleep, and for that, I was grateful. I needed to determine where we were and what was going on before she woke, assuming I could do so.

I vaguely remembered the voice that woke me.

Fated mate?

I must've been dreaming.

Our space pod—and that was the only way I could think of this thing we rode in—soared through the clouds and flung itself toward an enormous light purple landscape. It was only when we got closer that I realized we were traveling over water.

It flew lower. And lower, until I was sure I could touch the water if I stretched my hand down.

A large landmass a few miles across and made up of thick vegetation in varying shades of purple loomed ahead, and we plunged toward it. Before we could impact, the craft slowed. The low hum around us ceased, and we dropped, splashing down into the water a hundred feet away from the island.

Flora stirred and mumbled something about mermaids.

The glass overhead slid sideways and dropped, and fresh air poured into the small, tight space where we lay.

Cool water sloshed over the sides, waking Flora. Her eyes opened, and she frowned up at me. "Mommy?"

Something big and dark purple and with long fangs swam along the side of the spacecraft, its top fin breaking the surface of the water and its tail agitating behind it. As it passed, it smacked the small ship.

The pod flipped over.

Water gushed inside, upending it completely and dumping us out.

I clung to my daughter as we plunged into the vast purple sea.

CHAPTER 2
KHOL

Astorm would arrive in a handful of days, and I was fishing on shore, hoping to store plenty of meat to last me through the bad weather, when a gleaming object flew across the sky, aiming for the island I called home. The long, thin, silvery object splashed into the sea and the top slid to the side.

What could it be?

Before I could grab my bucket of fish, a wave rippled away from the cylinder, growing in volume and speed until it towered at least a Zuldrux warrior's height. It hit me where I stood with my feet planted in the sand and engulfed me, knocking me backward.

I righted myself and scrambled to collect my fish scattered on the shore. When I straightened, I swiped my wet hair from my eyes.

My wrist burned, and for one moment, I assumed something in the water had bitten me, but when I flipped my arm over, I gaped at the newly branded mark.

My heart seized. For three years, I'd mourned the mate the spirits gave me. I'd lost her, as I should. She was never mine, though I'd loved her. She'd belonged to a friend, and when someone murdered her because she cared for me, I'd given into my shame and left my clan forever. I traveled across the sea for days and when I found this uninhabited island, I built my home and resigned myself to living here by myself until the day I died and could join her.

The mating mark that proved she and I were meant for each other had faded after her death.

What could this new mark mean?

A wave. I lived here in harmony with a water spirit. Had the spirit decided I deserved a new fated mate?

No, no. I would never be worthy of another. My love for Weela had betrayed my best friend, and it had shamed me and my clan.

I did not deserve someone new.

However, there was no denying the mark gifted upon me by the water spirit.

Not long ago, a group of Zuldrux leaders traveled to a distant island in the middle of a lake to plead with our clan gods for mates. A disease had swept across our world ages ago, killing many, and now, few females were born. Our people were dying, and only the gods could save us. They agreed to send mates, and they said when a fated mate arrived, the male would be given a sign.

I, Khol, was traedor of the Taikeen Clan, though this was more a joke since I was the only member of this clan protected by a water spirit I refused to call a god.

But me, a mate? It couldn't be true. I'd loved one female, and I could never feel the same about another.

I stomped on the hope burning through my heart. After what happened, it wasn't right for me to dream of a happy future with a loving female by my side.

A shriek shot across the water, and I watched as the odd

craft drifted, plunging below the waves. An arm stabbed through the surface, telling me someone was in trouble.

Was this the mate the water spirit thought to send me?

When the fin of a sharpedeer arrowed in on the person, my low growl rang out. I might not be worthy of a mate, but I couldn't let her die.

With my coral knives in my palms, I dove into the water and swam toward her.

Hold on, I whispered in my mind. *I will save you.*

Before I could reach her, I dove down and opened my eyes to see what was happening. She had four legs and four arms, and her long, pale hair swirled around her thick body.

Until her body parted into two.

Two humans had been sent to Zuldruxia? But no, one was much smaller than the other, a youngling.

The larger one had two breasts, not the four seen in Zuldruxian females.

I bobbed back to the surface, pondering what I'd seen.

Her yelp rang out, and when she looked my way, I took in eyes as rich as soil, so different from the teal common among Zuldruxians.

A sharpedeer shot through the water, aiming right at her and the youngling.

With a snarl, I swam furiously toward them, slashing out at the sharpedeer with one of my blades, nicking its thick, scaled hide. Dark lavender blood slid from the wound, and the beast slashed out with its spiked tail to impale me.

I swung up with my blades, gouging into its soft belly, driving them to the hilt and twisting. Blood gushed from the wounds, and with a final swipe of its tail, the sharpedeer gave up and swam away quickly.

I turned to the human, determined to get her and the

youngling out of the water before we drew in another predator.

She must be the youngling's mother. A feverish joy shot through me, a feeling I needed to suppress. The water spirit may have gifted me with two precious beings, but they could never belong to me, not after what I'd done. Yet I couldn't leave them here. I could not make myself swim away.

I swam up beside the larger one and gave her a nod. My smile lifted. I couldn't help it. She was lovely. Human, like others I'd recently met. And beautiful beyond belief.

I could not accept her, but I wouldn't allow her to die, not like Weela.

"Welcome," I croaked, dipping my head toward her. "I'm Khol. I'll save you and the youngling."

CHAPTER 3
NANCY

A gorgeous, blue-skinned alien with silver hair and a muscular body one-and-a-half times my size wrapped his arms around me and lifted me out of the water.

His soft gaze went from me to Flora. "Hold on. I'll get you to shore."

"I can swim," I said. It wasn't that I didn't want his help, but if I'd learned nothing else over the past five years, it was that I needed to rely solely on myself.

No trusting anyone, not even a hot alien.

His unibrow ridge lifted. "But what about the youngling?"

Youngling? He must mean Flora.

"Thank you, but I can do this." I turned onto my back and started paddling with Flora draped across my chest. Why wasn't she waking up? She was breathing.

Those robocops better not have hurt her or I'd . . .

There was nothing I could do about it right now. They'd kidnapped me and dumped me in an alien world. I'd do all I could to find a way back, but with the tiny spaceship I'd arrived in sinking into the depths and more alien shark fins cutting through the water, heading my way, the odds of me returning to Earth were less than . . . Well, less than me surviving long enough to reach shore.

Khol kept pace with us, swimming easily while shooting glares toward the sharknados. He was attractive in an alien way, with a strong jawline and a slight beard, plus gorgeous dark blue eyes. I didn't know his intentions, but his eagerness to help me spoke well of him.

The small ship we'd arrived on disappeared beneath the water, taking our only chance of returning to Earth along with it. Even if I could bring it up from the bottom, would it function? I was no engineer. It was all I could do to drive a stick shift back home.

It looked like I was stuck on this planet for the foreseeable future.

A large fin rose above the water about thirty feet away, and the alien shark darted toward us at a feverish pace.

"We need to get out of the water," I cried, flailing toward shore with my arm snug around Flora snug in my arms.

With a growl, Khol intercepted the water beast, diving down to meet up with it before it could reach us.

The water boiled, and I should help him. He'd placed his own life in danger to protect mine and Flora's. But there was no way I could fight off alien sharks and keep my daughter from drowning. She couldn't swim, though lessons at the Y were on my agenda.

So much for my Earth agenda.

If I didn't keep moving toward shore, I'd risk both our lives. I didn't care about myself, not too much, but Flora would not survive on an alien planet alone.

Flora stirred, whimpering, turning onto her belly and

wrapping her arms around my neck. When she flailed, she shoved me beneath the surface. I kicked my legs, shooting our heads back up, and she coughed and started crying.

"It's okay, sweetie." I stroked her back, hoping she'd stop moving. "Hold still." The shore seemed too far away, though it couldn't be more than twenty feet.

If she kept struggling, we'd both drown.

As I held her with one arm while stretching the other out to drag us toward shore, I kept looking back.

Khol didn't come up for air, and a stark, sad feeling shot through me, as if I'd lost something precious. I tried to shrug it off, but it persisted as the water continued to churn in that area. A shark's tail whipped against the surface, its body twisting as it battled with the blue alien male who'd made himself our savior. Others swam closer, drawn by the fight.

His arm snapped above the water and his hand holding a blade dove back down. He came up for air before plunging below again. Water splashed, and a dark purple liquid swirled among the male and creature battling for their lives.

My feet hit sand, and I struggled up the sandy bank, clinging to my daughter.

Flora looked up at me. "Mommy?" she asked in a sleepy voice. "Time ta go to daycare?"

"Not right now, sweetie."

"Why are we wet?" Frowning, she peered around as I strode up the shore, shooting looks back at Khol. He hadn't come up again, but the water still churned. "Dis isn't daycare."

Anything but.

"We . . ." How could I explain this to a child? "We went swimming in a new place." I lowered her to her feet and held her shoulders, meeting her blue eyes she'd inherited from me. Her brown hair came from her dad, but her high cheekbones and petite frame were pure me. I adored every bit of her, however. He hadn't wanted her, but I did. "I need you to wait here."

Did I dare leave her alone?

I scanned the jungle about fifty feet away, and I didn't see anything lurking among the thick vegetation, but after what attacked us in the water, I'd be foolish to trust anything about this strange new world.

"Okay, Mommy." Still sleepy, Flora dropped down onto the sand and picked up a shell the size of her hand, frowning at it. "Pwetty."

"Yes, it's pretty. Stay here."

"Okay."

Most of the time, my daughter could win awards for being cooperative. Even the terrible twos hadn't been much more than a blip. She was an easygoing child, and as a single mom struggling to make ends meet, I was eternally grateful for that.

Would she do as I asked this time? I'd risk it, though I'd keep an eye on her while I tried to help Khol. I couldn't get rid of the feeling that I had to do what I could to save him.

I grabbed a piece of driftwood off the sand and spun, but before I could splash back into the water, Khol emerged from the waves like King Triton come to plunder on shore. For a moment, my heart thrilled, and it was all I could do not to swoon.

I'd fallen for a bad boy once and look where it got me—raising a child alone. I told myself I'd never give into a guy's dubious charms again. But damn. Khol could be featured on the cover of a magazine as *hot guy of the year*.

He was a drool-worthy hero in a TikTok video. Someone to fantasize about while lying alone in bed at night.

He wore only a dark purple loincloth that clung to his narrow hips and outlined a sizable bulge in the front, and water sluiced down his muscular chest and rippled along the defined grooves of his abs.

He was a Greek statue come to life. A portrait of manliness I could stare at forever.

My stick dropped from my limp hand, thudding on the sand by my feet, and I tried to drag my gaze away from him. Behind me, Flora chattered about the shells, the sand, the water, and who knows what else.

How could anyone expect me to think at a time like this?

He sheathed his blades at his waist as he strode toward me with complete confidence, as if he hadn't just defeated a creature who would've eaten me and Flora in one bite.

Behind him, the sharknados swarmed the carcass he left behind.

Stopping in front of me, he stared, taking in my face and my body, and it was only then that I realized I wore a white nightie and nothing else. The thin fabric clung to my skin, and the stiff wind made shivers erupt from deep inside me. My nipples beaded from the cold, and my body shook with spent adrenaline.

I should be afraid of this obviously virile alien male's interest, right? Instead, all I could do was stare at him with the same greedy gaze he used on me.

"Welcome to Zuldrux," he said in a husky, smooth voice. His throat worked with a deep swallow, and he flicked his gaze away from mine. "I will . . ." He trailed off, and I got the sudden impression he was shy.

"I'm Nancy," I said, grateful I could speak even if I couldn't think of much to say.

Flora got up and patted my leg. "Mommy. Mommy! Look what I got." She held up a pink shell the size of her fist. "Look, blue man. Look!"

"This is my daughter, Flora," I said, stroking her long, wet hair. She wore the same pink princess dress she'd insisted on wearing to daycare. Flora insisted all girls were royalty, and all royalty adored pink. Who could argue with something like that?

Khol stooped down in front of her and held out his hand.

"Pwetty," she said. Frowning, she poked his arm. "Blue. Mommy, I want blue skin too."

Her lower lip trembled, and she burst into tears.

CHAPTER 4

KHOL

Nancy's tiny youngling sat onto the ground and, tipping her head back, started shrieking.

"Oh, now . . ." I shot a glance Nancy's way. "Is she injured?" Why else would her eyes leak water? I wanted to enfold both her and Nancy in my arms and hold them. Tell them they were safe now, that I, Khol, would give my life to protect them.

I didn't dare. The water spirit was playing tricks on me, tempting me with a mate when I should live alone with my shame for the rest of my days.

"She's having a meltdown because her skin isn't blue," Nancy said with a wry twist of her mouth.

Melting . . . down? I peered around, but nothing was melting, though the sun was hot today.

I had almost no experience with younglings, but I understood fretful creatures. I'd rescued more than I could count since I built my house on this island.

Everyone understood kindness.

I sat beside Flora on the sand and pointed to the water. "Look," I said softly, watching to see what she'd do.

Flora's head lifted, and she stared at the white-capped lavender waves gliding up the shore before retreating into the sea.

"I wanna be blue," she said sadly. "Why can't I be blue?"

"Pink is lovely," I said, touching the skin on her arm. So soft and fragile, and the same skin color as Nancy.

"My daughter loves pink." Nancy said, tugging her long, very pale hair that rivaled the sunlight away from her neck, squeezing out the water. Her soil-brown eyes met mine before shooting to her youngling. "Everything pink."

"Could we have more pink?" I called out to the water spirit.

A wave rushed up the shore and when it retreated, it left a small pile of pink shells behind.

"Look at this," I told Flora, lifting one and holding it out to her. "Small creatures call this their home."

Flora blinked up at me, and I took in her pale blue eyes unlike the teal common in Zuldruxians, though mine were darker. Her brown hair hung in a lank band down her back, dripping water onto her pink gown unlike anything I'd seen before. An entire night sky of stars appeared to live in the tunic.

Such a sweet youngling. At least she'd stopped crying.

"Thank you. She needed a good distraction." Nancy peered around. "Where are we?"

While Flora examined the shell I'd laid on her lap, I rose, keeping my gaze trained on the water. "This is Zuldrux."

What was I supposed to do with a human female, let alone a human youngling? I never thought the gods would gift a mate to me, but here she was.

I couldn't claim her.

"Nice tattoo," she said, studying the mark on my arm.

When she traced her fingertip across the five-point pattern with dots near each point, it flared before fading to black lines once more. Gasping, she yanked her arm back and cupped her hand against her chest. "Touching it burned me."

"Look," I said, pointing at the hand she clung to.

She extended her arm, and her eyes widened. "Where did that come from? I don't have tattoos. I don't have any tattoos!" For a moment, I thought she'd flop on the sand and cry out like Flora just did. If so, should I give her a shell?

Instead, she raced into the water to her knees and dipped her hand in, scrubbing it. "What did you do to me?"

"A wave splashed over me right after you arrived," I said, joining her in the water, watching over her with a blade in my hand.

"Rogue waves aren't uncommon."

"Here, they are."

"Do you have earthquakes and tsunamis on Zuldrux?"

I shook my head, though I wasn't sure what either of those things were. "This is the first rogue wave I've seen. The marks mean . . ."

Pausing in her washing, she frowned up at me. "What?"

"See . . . the spirit . . ."

Her frown deepened. She stopped trying to wash it off, which was good because it would remain for the rest of her life. Straightening, she rubbed her lower back, her frown remaining. "Spirit?"

"My clan spirit is one of water. I refuse to call them gods."

She blinked a few times. "Okay."

"We begged . . . Alright, I *personally* didn't beg. I never would. But the other traedors did. My clan spirit hadn't been worshiped in a very long time, so they're . . . unruly."

Water splashed hard against my thighs, the spirit telling me they didn't like my comment.

"Let's leave the water, and I'll try to explain," I added.

Nancy scowled at the sea before she turned and walked beside me up the shore. We stopped beside Flora, who kept scooping up sand in the shell I'd given her before dumping it out to form a pile.

"Is it safe to remain here?" Nancy asked, her intent gaze scanning the jungle.

"So far."

Her skin quivered. "So far?" Her hand jutted toward Flora. "Come on, sweetie. We need to find a place to hide."

"Oh, I'll protect you." I showed her my coral blade while pressing my fist against my chest. "I swear."

"You and your water spirit, I assume."

Did I hear sarcasm in her voice? No, it couldn't be. Unless she was like many Zuldruxians who'd forsaken the gods, abandoning them long, long ago.

A hoarse bellow rang out in the jungle.

A jolt shot through Nancy. She scooped up her youngling and bolted along the shore.

I took off after her.

CHAPTER 5
NANCY

"Why are we running?" Khol asked, jogging beside me. He'd returned his knife to the sheath at his waist when he should keep it handy for whatever might attack next.

"Something's hunting us," I cried out, tripping as I ran with Flora in my arms. I was used to carrying her to bed if she fell asleep on the sofa. Picking her up if she was hurt. But I'd never gone for a run with her in my arms, and I was nearly worn out already.

"Nothing on this island will harm you," Khol said, pacing along beside us without a break in his wind. Truly, his gorgeous muscular-ness wasn't fair. It gave him an advantage.

"Something bellowed in the jungle. It's after us."

He shot a glance that way. "That was a trikee. A kind of bird. It's tiny, but it has a loud shriek."

I slowed to a fast walk, shooting wild looks at the thick jungle to my left. "You're sure it was only a bird?"

He nodded. "I am."

Flora wiggled. "Down. Down, Mommy."

Almost from the time my daughter could walk, she'd wanted to do everything under her own steam. Since I valued independence, I encouraged her to test the world around her as often as I could. When I lowered her to her feet, she peered around. "Where my shell?" Her gaze sought Khol's. "Where my shell?"

"Water spirit?" he said softly, following the words with a hum.

A wave splashed up the shore, leaving a big pink shell behind as it flowed back down the bank.

Coincidence. That was all this was.

Khol walked over and scooped it up, handing it to Flora, who proceeded to sit and start working on a new sandcastle, something we'd done whenever we went to the beach.

He shot me a sweet smile that made my bones melt. He had tusks. Real, thumb-sized tusks jutting up from his lower jaw. What did he rip into with them? I wasn't sure I dared ask.

"Water spirits don't exist," I said.

His smile faded. "I can understand not believing. I, myself, didn't believe at first. But . . ." His gaze drifted to the sea. "After a time, this one convinced me."

Chills rippled across my skin. "Tell me everything."

He gave me a slow nod. "Let me take you to where you'll feel safe, and then I'll answer all your questions."

I gave him a long look. He wouldn't be the first guy to try to lure me to "a safe place" where I'd be anything but.

Only pure kindness shone in his pretty blue eyes, and I shouldn't be softening just because he was attractive.

But he hadn't made any threatening gestures—so far.

"Alright," I finally said.

"Would you like to go to my home, Flora?" he asked, extending his hand.

"I'll take her," I said, thrusting my hand beside his.

Flora got up and, with the shell clutched against her chest, she took Khol's hand, smiling up at him. "I like blue man, Mommy."

He shot me a smile before turning and leading my daughter into the jungle.

I trotted behind them, still unsure about all this. He'd come across as friendly, but I was taken advantage of once and my heart would need convincing before I'd willingly trust anyone else again.

As we walked along a narrow trail, I fluffed the front of my nightie. Without the ocean breeze, the air hung with humidity and sweat coiled down my spine.

Sunlight filtered through the dense canopy overhead made up of purples with only a few touches of green, pink, and yellow, the latter colors, big flowers. Dappled patterns danced on the forest floor as we walked, and vines draped lazily from towering trees, their trunks at least three of my arm's length around. Birds chattered in the distance, and a few lavender creatures the size of squirrels with darker purple, fluffy tails leaped from one branch to the next as if they needed to keep up to watch us.

A few insects zipped past, much too busy with whatever they were doing to pay us any mind. I hadn't seen a mosquito, but where there was water and tropical weather, I'd find them. Or they'd find me. They loved to bite me in particular.

Flora chattered, pointing at this flower and that, and even I, who was used to her lisp, couldn't understand half of what she said.

Khol listened to her raptly, pausing to show her tiny flowers growing beneath broad leaves, and even stooping down to make sure she saw a large, purple insect much like a praying mantis clinging to the end of a vine.

He really was kind. And so far, not a creep like some men. He'd still bear watching.

I kept rubbing the star-shaped tattoo I'd picked up during my travels. Why did it match the one on Khol's arm? It had to be a coincidence. I was mistaken. *Mine* had not appeared right after I touched his.

Though I hadn't seen it until then.

"Look, Mommy," Flora said, pointing to one of the pink, fluffy-tailed creatures perching on a stump about ten feet away inside the thicker jungle on our right. "A kitty."

"Not quite, though it's cute, isn't it?"

She was tired, which made her lisp more pronounced. I'd have to continue the speech therapy she'd started on Earth until we could return, and she could attend again.

There I went, assuming we would be stuck here for a while, let alone that we'd find our way home.

"We're almost there," Khol said, pointing toward the trail ahead.

As we walked in that direction, a low rush echoed around us, followed by a steady roar as we got closer.

Sunlight bloomed as we stepped out into a small meadow with a stone building nestled near the woods on the right and a wide stream with a series of falls on the left.

"Beautiful," I breathed, taking in the jungle beyond, the sparkle of sunlight on the lavender water, and the falls flowing over long spans of ledge before plunging into a wide pool at the bottom. "Fresh water?" The sea here was as salty as the one back home.

"Yes. Plus plenty of fish and tubers," Khol said, gazing toward the stream. "Are you hungry?"

My belly rumbled to give him an answer.

"I want chicken nuggets," Flora said. "And mac 'n cheese. And a donut."

Khol's smile curled as he looked her way. "What about fish and tubers?"

"Donut." Flora's lower lip trembled, and tears threatened in her eyes. "Mac 'n cheese. Chicken nuggets."

"She has a great appetite," I said. "I'm sure she'll enjoy whatever you serve."

"No donut?" Flora's voice croaked, and her eyes swam. "Like choc-o-late donuts."

Didn't we all?

"Let's go with Khol and see what he has," I said brightly, hoping to divert an incoming storm. "I'm sure we'll enjoy whatever it is."

"Wait here," Khol said.

Before I could speak, he left us, bolting across the meadow and disappearing through the front door of the small house. Bangs rang out, followed by a screech, as if he was dragging heavy furniture around.

He emerged with a smile and strode over to stand with us, waving toward the building. "If you'll follow me."

"Nothing sneaky," I said, as if my words could keep something like that from happening.

His smile just widened.

We followed him across the meadow, Flora a touch sullen and me with a hesitant step. Inside the front door, I took in the large open area made up of a living room with a normal-appearing—though Khol-sized—couch, a few chairs and low tables, plus a kitchen area with a window along the back. Two doors exited on the left, and he led us to the first, swinging the panel wide.

"Flora can sleep here," he said with a flourish.

He'd piled things in one corner, creating a small open

space with a toddler-sized flat piece of furniture topped with a thick layer of blankets.

"Dis my bed?" Flora asked, curiosity nudging aside her quest for donuts.

"I hope you'll be comfortable here," he said.

She hopped up on it and sat, laying her shell on the improvised blanket pillow at the top. "Not napping," she said.

"We'll see," I said. We needed to get out of our wet things and eat. But it was clear she'd soon need a power nap to recharge her batteries.

"You can sleep in the other room," Khol said shyly, backing from the tiny room.

I followed him to the other room, where he gestured to the enormous bed, neatly made up with blankets. A low table sat to the right of the head of the bed, and a tall wardrobe had been placed on the left side of the room, beside the only window.

"I often bathe in the stream, but there's an area with a . . ." Color rose into Khol's face. "A place for excrement through there."

Only now did I note a door to the left of the head of the bed.

It was clear Khol was going out of his way to make us feel welcome. And it was equally clear this was *his* bed. For some reason, the thought of him giving us these rooms when he didn't know where he'd sleep tonight made me want to cry.

It was nearly Christmas back home. Here? For all I knew, it was March, assuming Zuldrux kept track of months and named them. I shouldn't feel so sad about a missed holiday.

I sniffed and was grateful Flora had remained in her

room. I couldn't break down in front of my daughter; that would only scare her. As the adult, I needed to carry all our fear myself. But, damn, I was scared about this unknown situation, this unknown world, and okay, this unknown alien male standing politely by my side.

To think my biggest worry back on Earth was whether or not I could give my little girl a wonderful Christmas.

I could use a hug right about now.

A visit from Santa.

And, okay, a box full of chocolate donuts.

CHAPTER 6
KHOL

"I'll prepare a meal," I said, backing from the room. "You can get settled."

Her shrill laugh rang out. "I don't have anything to settle." Her hand swept toward her body I was struggling all the time not to gape at. Her thin white gown barely covered her slender legs. And the way the wet fabric molded her frame kept drawing my attention. The light in her eyes when she looked at her youngling daughter made my heart spasm.

She was supposed to be my new mate. Despite believing I wasn't worthy of one, the water spirit would say I should claim her.

No, no. I'd never do it. I didn't deserve someone in my life even if I was so lonely, my heart had hollowed out to a blank, empty thing.

But even more, I couldn't stand the look of distress on her face. This was something I could help her with.

"Tell the water spirit what you need," I said. "What Flora needs."

"How about dry clothing?" The words jerked out of her,

followed by another laugh that was much too shrill. "Toiletries. A Christmas tree and the presents . . ." As with Flora earlier, water brimmed in her eyes. "The presents I had ready to place beneath the tree."

"What is a griss-maas tree?" Could a shell be considered a present? I'd do anything to take away the sadness in her eyes, to make her feel better, even rush into the sea and collect an armload of pink shells if that would please her.

"Christmas is a holiday we celebrate where I come from. It has religious meaning. Mostly, it's a time of year when we reset ourselves, where we remember the value of being with those we love and dream of world peace." Her lips curved up before dropping downward, and she swiped at the wetness trickling from her eyes.

The water meant she was *sad*. Only now did I realize this.

"And how does a tree come into that?" I asked carefully. Could I help her with this? The water spirit would give her clothing and toil-ek-trees, whatever they were. I hoped they'd deliver those, that is. I'd ask them. If nothing else, it would distract me from the thought that the water spirit felt I should have a new mate.

"Part of the tradition is bringing a tree in from outside, though I used a fake one because I hate vacuuming up needles. They linger everywhere. I swear I still suck them up in June."

She sucked up needles?

Confused but wanting to help her feel better, I nodded. Speaking about this appeared to be slowing the sad water flow from her eyes.

"We decorate the tree and then we put presents beneath it," she said.

"This is griss-maas?"

"Christmas is the name of the special day. The tree's just part of the way we celebrate, as are presents. I'd planned everything. Christmas was supposed to take place in a few days, though for all I know, it's July and a thousand years later, so the days no longer matter. Robocops stole us from Earth, and they stole our lives along with it. I was picking Flora up from daycare when they grabbed us. They stuffed us inside a spaceship and brought us here, where they dumped us."

I was beginning to understand. Not everything about griss-maas, but how the gods brought her and Flora here. I wanted to soothe Nancy's sadness, because it was clear she was distressed. Like the other human women, she was stolen from her world—with a youngling, no less—and dropped here as if her own needs didn't matter.

"Water spirit?" I asked, lifting my voice. "Could you give Nancy and Flora clothing?"

A pile of neatly folded items lifted up through the floor. When I first settled here, it was a challenge obtaining needed things. But after I channeled water from the stream, guiding it underneath my house, the water spirit heard me and responded.

Nancy gasped and reeled away from the pile.

"They're for you," I said.

She took a step toward them and tentatively lifted the first thing off the pile, shaking it out to reveal a pale purple tunic that would fit her perfectly.

"The water spirit tends to select colors that blend with our sea," I said. The pants beneath the tunic had been made in a slightly darker lavender color. "You'll get used to it eventually." She'd have to. If nothing else, the island gods had made it clear they wouldn't send the women back to their home planet. "The spirit enjoys purple, pink, green, and a few shades of blue. I've been unable to get them to give me anything in brown or black. Or yellow, for that matter, though that surprises me the most since the sunlight hitting the water looks that color." I was rambling, something I did when I was nervous, but her uncertainty had spread to me, and I wasn't sure how to handle it.

"You're suggesting a water spirit gave me this clothing?" she asked, clearly skeptical.

"Don't the spirits give you what you need on . . . Earth?" One of the human women also mentioned the name of their home planet, though I'd forgotten it until Nancy named it.

Why would they name their world after soil? It had been a great mystery since I heard the term.

I'd traveled with my clan to the gathering, where I'd seen other human women lying in pods, waiting to be delivered to their fated mates. I'd met those who'd already fallen in love with Zuldruxian males.

I just never thought they'd send one to me.

This must be a mistake, and they'd soon tell me and take Nancy away to send her somewhere new.

My throat choked off at the thought, but this was how it should be. I did not deserve a new mate.

"If our god or gods are watching," she said, "they rarely make themselves known. Not even at Christmas, which is actually a holiday to celebrate a god."

Interesting. "Here, the spirits, as I choose to call them, listen, and if they can help, they do."

Her hand flicked out as if she was brushing aside my statement, but she'd soon see. I couldn't believe her planet's spirits didn't do things for her like they would here.

"The spirit has gifted you with clothing," I said. "And I'm sure they'll help with everything else. Just ask."

Nancy frowned. "Yeah. Sure. Tell me where the clothing came from."

"I already explained. When you remove what you wear at the end of the day, toss the items onto the floor and the spirit will reclaim it."

"If I've learned anything else in life, it's that no one picks up after me. If I want something done, I have to do it myself, so I won't be throwing my clothing onto the floor." She stooped down and dragged the pile to the side and pawed at the wooden floor I'd crafted myself from trees I dropped and formed into boards. "I can't figure out where the pile of clothes came from."

"One day, you'll become comfortable with this. Honestly, it took me time to accept it as well. I grew up with stone gods crafting meals and generating clothing for me. It took some time to get used to a water spirit."

"This makes no sense," she said, her forehead tightening.

"Others have said the same thing. As for griss-maas, I'll help you with that." I wasn't sure the spirit could do this for her, and even if they could, I wanted to be the one gifting her with something she clearly needed.

Continuing to touch the floor, she absently nodded. "Okay."

I backed out of the room. "Dress in something new. If you don't like what the spirit delivered, tell them what you need, and they'll do all they can to gift it to you."

"Things like this don't happen." She straightened, her head tilting toward me standing in the open doorway, before her gaze shifted. Her gasp rang out.

"Look, Mommy. I's a pwincess." Flora danced into the room, dressed in a new, pale green gown that fluffed out around her ankles. The water spirit had covered the garment with tiny sparkling pink shells.

Flora pirouetted in front of her mother, who clutched the bedpost as if she worried she'd fall.

Nancy's gaze met mine. "Water spirit?" she croaked.

I flashed her a smile and nodded. "Water spirit."

CHAPTER 7

NANCY

This wasn't possible. I didn't believe in magic, and honestly, I wasn't sure I completely believed in gods, let alone spirits, though I'd always hoped there was someone out there watching over us, maybe even guiding us.

But water spirits who delivered clothing at our request? Not happening.

Yet my daughter now wore a dry, green gown much like a princess would in a Disney movie.

She twirled around. "I's pwetty, right Mommy?"

I stooped down and held her arms, bringing her dance to a halt. "Where did you get the dress?"

"Da floor," she said, flaring the skirt and smiling down at the tiny shells adorning the fabric. "Pink and gween. Pwetty."

"You *are* pretty, sweetie." I released her, straightening. Flora spun and sang about princesses in a lilting voice while I frowned at Khol. "This can't be true." Yet . . . Yet . . . "Tell me more about this water spirit."

"Change out of your wet clothing," he said in a gentle

voice that made me feel melty. "I'll prepare a meal, though the house spirit will help. Join me, and while we eat, I'll explain."

"This better be good."

He flashed another smile that made my heart thump like horses galloping along the shore. "It will be very good."

He didn't mean anything sexual by the comment; I could tell that by the way he smiled and the kindness in his eyes. But my body heated just the same, coming to a low simmer when it shouldn't. He'd rescued me. He was giving us rooms inside his house to ensure Flora and I were comfortable. And now he was going to cook lunch. Breakfast. Dinner. Whatever the meal might be.

But he wasn't suggesting that he wanted anything else from me.

Why did that thought make me sad?

I wasn't *that* attracted to him, was I?

Okay, maybe a little. But my ex burned me, and it would take more than sweet smiles and a bit of kindness to make me let down my guard.

"Alright." There was no harm in changing out of this wet dress. Eating. Listening to what he had to say.

I also needed to wash off the mark on my hand.

"Would you like to help me make dinner?" he asked Flora, holding out his hand.

She twirled over to him and bowed. "I's a pwincess. I's don't cook."

His laugh rang out. "Then you can sit nearby and give me direction while your mother changes."

"Alright." She took his hand and danced beside him as he shut the door. Their footsteps retreated.

Since I was an overprotective mom, I rushed to the door, cracked it open, and watched as he led Flora into the small kitchen area. He placed her on the table with her legs dangling.

"Don't wiggle or you'll fall," he said softly. "Promise?"

"I pwomise," she chirped.

"What do you want for dinner?"

"Chicken nuggets. Mac 'n cheese. Donuts!" The swing of her legs punctuated each item.

"Fish and tubers?" he asked with a grin.

"Yucky."

His grin widened. "Are you sure? I think they taste amazing."

She crossed her arms on her chest and scowled. "Fish is yucky."

"Hmm." He tapped his chin, looking comically huge standing next to my petite daughter. "Let me see if we can create what you want."

"Okay."

"Don't fall."

"I won't, Khol. Pwomise."

He backed away and turned to the counter, though he kept an eye on her. If she so much as started to slide off the table, he'd scoop her up and hold her in his arms.

I suspected he'd give his own life to protect her.

That was good enough for me.

With new tears in my eyes, I shut the door and turned back to frown at the pile of clothing.

"I'd like a sundress," I said firmly. "Tea length. Sleeveless. Tank style will do. A flared skirt, though not as wide as what you made for Flora. White with . . . yellow flowers." Was I out of my mind to ask for something like this from a "water spirit"?

Nah, I was testing this out, not expecting anything to happen.

A folded item oozed up from the floor beside the pile I'd shifted.

I blinked at it, expecting it to disappear. There was no such thing as house spirits giving a person clothing. I'd imagined the other items appearing earlier. They were stacked beneath the bed and Khol had . . . somehow slid them out from beneath with his foot when I wasn't looking. They just happened to look about my size. He had a smaller friend who wasn't here right now.

Or maybe all of this *was* real.

Had his water spirit played a role in bringing me and my daughter here, and if so, why?

"Dress," I told myself. "Go out there and get your answer from Khol. Ignore how cute he is, how nice he is to Flora, how eager he appears to want to please you. It's a front he's put on to lull you. Once you succumb, like you did with Richard, jerk that he is, Khol will start showing his true colors and they won't be pretty. Then you can walk away and form a new life on this alien planet with your daughter."

With that, I lifted the dress from the floor. White, but with purple flowers.

Oh yeah, Khol said the water spirit used limited colors, and they couldn't do yellow.

Green worked.

I scurried into the bathroom and after I finally figured out how to make water rush from the sort-of sink, I scrubbed and scrubbed at the mark on my hand. It didn't come off, but I'd keep trying.

It was just a coincidence that it matched Khol's.

Dressed, I emerged from the room to find plates on the table and Flora sitting on a tall, Flora-sized chair, digging into her meal.

Khol leaned against the counter, watching her eat with a big smile on his face. He shouldn't do that all the time, because it made my heart skip and heat flare deep inside me. It also made me want to throw away my inhibitions and climb all over him.

No can do. Only pain lay in that direction.

And unexpected pregnancies. It wasn't like the robo-cops had tucked a pack of Khol-sized condoms into the space pod they'd used to send me here.

"What are you eating?" I asked Flora as I stopped beside the table. It looked like her favorite food, but it couldn't be.

"Chicken nuggets." She pointed to the pale lavender chunks on one side of the plate. "Mac 'n cheese." Her finger traced across the top of the pasta-appearing, cheese-coated mound near the nugget. "And a donut."

The donut looked like the chocolate one I used to buy as a treat on Sunday, but it couldn't be real. This was an alien planet.

Khol came over to stand beside me, and why did he smell so yummy? I caught a hint of something like spicy ginger, fresh air, sunshine, and another scent I couldn't place. He'd swam in the sea, just like me, and I didn't smell anywhere near as good. My hair was sticky from the salt, and I was going to need a tube of deodorant soon. Could the water spirit provide something like that?

He leaned close and whispered, his words teasing across my ear. "It's grains and tubers, but the water spirit formed them into her favorite treats. It makes Flora happy, and if nothing else, my water spirit wants us to smile."

"This isn't possible." Yet, here I stood, wearing a sundress that had oozed up from the wooden floorboards.

Perhaps the best thing to do was just roll with it until I could determine the exact cause.

"I asked the water spirit to prepare a meal for you as well," he said. Before I could say a peep, he swept me up and placed me in another big chair. My chin could rest on the table's surface without me leaning forward. "Water spirit?"

The world rumbled beneath me, the chair stretching up and shrinking at the same time.

I yelped and leaped out of it, backing away from it while Flora laughed and pointed.

"Funny, Mommy."

"What did you do?" I snarled at Khol.

"The chair was too big for you."

"Yes, but—"

"The house spirit made it smaller." He cracked another smile that chipped away at the wall I kept trying to build around my heart. "If you'd prefer to sit in the large one, just say so."

"No, um . . . No. This is okay." I tentatively went over and sat in the chair again, noting how it had shrunk to fit me perfectly. "My name isn't Goldilocks," I called to the room in general. "Despite my hair color."

I swore a low hum rang out.

Khol settled in the third chair that fit him perfectly already. "Your name is Nancy."

"The name comes from a story," I blurted out. "She has golden locks or hair. There are three bears. Chairs that don't fit. Food that's . . ." The plate holding what had previously looked like rice and chunks of potatoes slid closer to me, only now the food resembled what Flora kept shoveling into her mouth.

She hummed and wiggled with happiness, eating better than she had in months. "Yummy."

"This is overwhelming," I told Khol weakly.

"I agree."

"Has this always been your home?"

"No. I've only been here a short time. I used to live on one of the floating islands, but left, resigning myself to . . ." He cleared his throat and dragged his gaze away from mine. "I like solitude."

"Which we've disrupted."

"I don't mind. I like having you and Flora here."

"Give us a minute, and you might change your mind."

The mark on his arm flared, and a burning feeling seared across the back of *my* hand. I gaped down as the matching symbol rippled with tiny sparks. "What's happening?" Again, I erupted from my chair, backing away with my hand clutched to my chest. I didn't stop until I ran into the sofa. "You did something to it."

"The water spirit caused this." He nudged his head to my chair. "Sit, and I'll explain."

"I's done." Flora slid off the chair, and grabbing her plate, brought it over to place on the counter, like I'd taught her.

Who washed the dishes here? The water spirit?

Shrill laughter bubbled up my throat, and I worried if I didn't hold it back, I'd be rolling on the floor, shrieking while crying for the rest of my life.

That would go over well with my daughter. I was supposed to be the strong person here. The parent who made sure she was safe and secure.

Flora's plate sunk into the wooden counter, disappearing.

I slumped onto the sofa, done with this world for the moment.

CHAPTER 8
KHOL

While Flora skipped to her room to play, I sunk onto the sofa beside Nancy and laid her plate on her lap.

"Eat," I said firmly. "Then we'll talk."

I'd explain and assure her I wouldn't expect her to truly mate with me, and she'd . . . Probably leave me, as she should. I could take her to shore and help her find a new clan to settle with. Her mark would fade like the one from my first mate had, and she'd find someone new.

I'd continue with my lonely isolation on this island.

She mechanically lifted her eating implement and started placing food in her mouth, chewing slowly and swallowing before adding another bite. Once she'd finished, I took her plate to the counter and brought her the drink I'd requested from the house spirit, placing it in her hand.

"You must be thirsty." I watched while she drank. Once she'd placed the empty cup on the table in front of the sofa, I sighed. "As I said, I came here to start a new life. Actually, I discovered this island while fishing and decided to stay."

"Why did you need to start a new life?"

"I . . ." Did I dare explain? "I had a female I adored, but she died."

"Oh, I'm terribly sorry." She turned my way, her face full of concern. "What happened?"

"She was murdered for loving me."

Nancy's breath caught. "I don't understand."

And I didn't want to tell her the entire story. She'd think as poorly of me as I did myself. She'd reject me as she should.

Which meant I had to tell her.

"I grew up in the Dastalon Clan, the sky clan with stone gods," I said. "Though I secretly called them spirits as well."

"I don't . . . None of that makes sense. Sky clan?"

"The clan lives on floating islands, and they take to the sky riding huge birds. Stone spirits protect and serve the clan."

"Like your water spirit."

"Yes." My smile flashed, and her gaze focused on my mouth, which sent a strange thrill through me. I was attracted to Nancy. She'd already brought hope to my world even if I didn't deserve it. "Growing up, I was good friends with a male named Nevarn. We did everything together. Weela was one of the young females in the clan. As adults, her parents and his grandfather arranged for them to mate."

"Which must be like marriage back on Earth."

"Yes." I'd heard one of the women use that term. "Nevarn and Weela didn't love each other, but they did as they were told."

"That's too bad. There are arranged marriages on Earth, and while some of the couples find happiness with each other, others don't."

"So it was with Nevarn and Weela. She and I were friends but . . ."

"Ah," she said, her face clearing. "You two fell in love?"

I turned my arm to reveal the new symbol. "One day, while we walked together, a matching mating mark appeared on both of our arms. This meant we were true mates and fated to love each other."

"But she was with Nevarn." Nancy rubbed my arm in sympathy, and I should not allow the heat I felt from her simple touch to flare through me.

"We fought it, of course, but eventually, we gave in. Such is the way of true mating. We . . . weren't intimate, but we might as well have been because we betrayed Nevarn in our hearts."

"You said she was murdered?" A mask fell over her features, and she would no longer meet my eye.

"Nevarn was accused of killing her. I thought he found out about us and did it, but recently, it was proven that her parents killed her."

Nancy's gasp rang out. "How could parents murder their child?"

"Out of spite and anger. They discovered she and I were in love, and they feared the clan finding out. Once we discovered they'd murdered her, they were banished and I . . ." Now I had to look away. I could not meet Nancy's eyes. "I left my clan, banishing myself. After finding this island, I built my home and resigned myself to living here alone forever."

"And now my daughter and I are here, messing with your atonement."

"Atonement?" An interesting way to look at it.

"It sounds to me like you and Weela fought your feelings. You fell in love, but sometimes, that can't be avoided.

She died, so I'd say you both paid the ultimate price. Do you feel you need to make amends for falling in love?"

"I do."

"Did Nevarn say this, or did you tell this to yourself?"

"He forgave me." I stared at my hands clasped in my lap. "I don't deserve to be with others. I hurt my friend. I hurt Weela. If I'd stayed away from her, she'd still be alive."

"If Nevarn forgave you, and you're paying the price you set for yourself, why can't you forgive yourself?"

"I'm the reason she was killed."

"I can understand blaming yourself. I'd do the same thing."

"I felt you needed to know this."

She tapped the mark on my arm. "Is this the mating mark from Weela?"

I shook my head. "That faded after she died. This one appeared when I saw you."

"Which means . . ." Her sigh rang out. "I can't believe all this yet . . ." Her fingertip traced along the pattern on the back of her hand.

"I won't try to claim you."

"That's good, because I don't want anyone to claim me. I had my chance at love like you, and it's gone. I don't need another."

"The one you adored died like Weela?"

"No, um, he's still alive." She leaned back on the cushions. "Tell me why your water spirit brought me here."

A change of subject, but I understood the pain of losing someone. Her mate might not have died, but I sensed they were no longer together before she was brought here. If she wanted me to know why, she'd tell me.

"Long ago," I said, "ships much larger than the one you arrived in landed on this planet. Beings came out of the ship, and some sank into the ground, erupting back out in enormous crystal forms. Others flew through the air and landed on islands that float above the sea where they fused with the stone support system—"

"You mentioned floating islands. All islands float in the sea."

"These hover in the sky, far above the sea."

Her low laugh rang out, fading quickly. "That's not possible."

"Yet it's true. I'll show you sometime."

"Where did the other gods go?"

"They scattered themselves in the sand of the vast deserts some distance from here," I said. "Others merged with the trees."

"This sounds like something from a sci-fi movie."

I wasn't sure what she meant, but I nodded. Any way she could translate what happened into something she understood would help her accept the life she'd find here on Zuldrux.

"My people lived in harmony with these people they called gods," I said.

"Ah, the ones you call spirits," she said. "I bet they're aliens from a different world."

"You're the alien here." I frowned. "And I guess you could say they are too, since they didn't originally come from here. Most call them gods. But we didn't live peacefully together forever. A disease swept across our world, killing many of those who'd come here, plus many Zuldruxians. The gods were blamed, and the people fled the lives they'd formed with them. Time passed, and my people started to die. Few younglings were born, and most were male."

"This definitely sounds like a sci-fi movie." She turned

on the sofa to face me, hitching her leg up beneath her sweet bottom I ached to touch. At least her face appeared open, and she was willing to listen to me. "Go on."

"Some Zuldruxians returned to the spirits and lived among them once more."

She peered around. "And yours?"

"As I said, my spirit is that of water." I could tell she didn't understand, though she would. "My clan is small and contains only one person. Me." My face heated. Would she scorn me for forming a new clan? I felt I should, that I needed to belong *somewhere* even if I wasn't worthy of a life among others. "The Taikeen Clan. At the recent clan gathering, I offered others space on this island, and some Zuldruxians expressed interest. Life is different here, and some suggested it might be nice to help build a new clan into a thriving community. No one has ventured here so far, however."

Maybe if some did, I could find a person to love. Weela would want that, just as I'd want it for her if I'd died.

Why, then, did I hesitate to accept the gift the water spirit gave me in Nancy?

"It's a worthy goal," she said. "How big is this island?"

"It takes two days to walk across it."

"Wow. That's miles long. And you live here all by yourself?"

"So far. After we rejoined the spirits, our lives improved due to what they offered, but our people are still dying. A few traedors, which means clan leaders, went to the central spirits who live on an island within a lake, to plead for intervention."

"I sense this is where my daughter and I come in, though I'm eager to find out specifically how."

"The traedors asked the island spirits to give them mates."

Nancy's shoulders sagged. "Spirits. Mates. Robocops stealing . . . my daughter and I from Earth. It doesn't make sense."

I nodded. "You're not the first female from Earth to arrive here."

"Wait. What? Where are they?" She stared around.

"Some wait in their pods while others have been gifted to Zuldruxians."

"We're not yours to be given away," she pointed out quietly. "I doubt any of us were willing to be kidnapped and brought here to be dumped in some guy's lap."

"It's true. None of the women were glad to be here—at first."

"And now?"

"Three have mated with Zuldruxian males and they're happy."

"So you say."

"They've told me this. I recently traveled to meet with others at the clan gathering, and human women arrived with their mates. They're in love. Some are expecting younglings."

"I won't believe this unless I can see it."

"I'll take you to them soon, then, because I want you to know that it's true. You're safe here, both you and Flora. The gods brought you here for a purpose."

She frowned at the mark on her hand. "To serve as your mate?"

"I've told you I would not claim you. I'm not worthy of another mate."

Sadness flickered across her face. "I don't want a mate either, so we're even on that. Where does that leave me?"

"I . . ." I pinched my eyes shut. "I can take you to one of the bigger clans. Vanessa is mated to Aizor, the traedor of the Indigan Clan. It will take many days to journey across the land and through the forest, but I'll take you there, and you can settle with them."

And I'd return to my lonely existence here on this island, the only life I deserved.

"Alright." Her brow furrowed, and she studied the mark on her hand. "If we go our separate ways, will the spirits remove the mark like they did after Weela was killed?"

"Perhaps. I don't know what they'll do." Scorn me, most likely, and that was all I could accept. "Until we can leave the island, I'll care for you and do my best to make sure you and Flora are happy. A storm is coming, and once it has passed, I'll take you to the others. If you wish to remain with them rather than me, I'll step away." I suspected my heart would break once more, but how could I force this precious female to remain with me?

"Tell me more about this tattoo." She traced her finger along the pattern and tiny lights flared beneath her skin once more.

Why would the gods do this to us? It wasn't fair to Nancy, and it placed something unobtainable in front of me. I couldn't claim her. I didn't deserve to claim her.

"True matings are rare even among Zuldruxians," I said.

"I sense a touch of permanency in your statement."

If I truly believed in the will of the spirits, I'd know that we were destined to love for this lifetime and beyond. But that couldn't be true.

I'd loved Weela, and she was murdered.

I couldn't risk falling for Nancy and having something horrible happen to her as well.

I was doomed to love and lose.
Weela.
And I would bet anything that I'd lose Nancy as well.

CHAPTER 9
NANCY

It kind of made sense if I didn't try to analyze it. The aliens living on this planet found a way to hijack robocops and the spaceship heading to Mars. I suspected the robocops kidnapped a bunch of women and brought them here as gifts for Zuldruxian warriors.

Were other women waking up and finding themselves lost in a new world with males who were eager to call them "true mates"? Although, Khol was pretty much rejecting me, just like Richard had back on Earth when I told him I was pregnant.

Khol had loved someone and lost her just like me, and if anything, that should draw us together. But even if I wanted to be with him, how could I compete with someone he'd not only loved and lost, but who was also his fated mate?

Unless I believed I was now his new fated mate.

People deserved to be happy. We muddled through life, doing our best, but having someone standing by your side, someone who was proud to be with you, who cared for you, was priceless.

Could Khol be that person for me?

I wasn't sure, and I certainly didn't need to decide anything like that now.

Even if I dared try again with Khol, there was no guarantee he'd ever want me. His rejection would suck as much if not more than when Richard walked out of my life.

I swallowed hard. "I don't know what I want to do." I was safe here; this I knew in my heart. Khol would never hurt me or Flora.

But how could I accept being gifted to an alien, especially one who was making it clear he didn't want me?

Through the window, I could see it had gotten dark. The world kept spinning, faster and faster, hauling me along with it. I wasn't sure what to make of this, but exhaustion kept dragging down my mind, making it hard to think.

"You're tired," he said, rising. "You should sleep. We can talk more in the morning. I have an idea."

Normally, I might be curious to hear his idea, but right now, I could barely stay awake.

"I'll put Flora to bed." I said. "Do you have any toothbrushes we can use? Nightgowns?" Though I could wear the white thing I'd arrived in if it was dry. Flora would probably want to wear the shell princess gown to bed, but I'd talk her into something else. Maybe one of the tunics the water spirit left me.

"I'll sleep out here." He waved to the couch. "I don't know what toof-brushes are, however."

"I always floss and brush my teeth before bed."

"Ah." He nodded, though a frown creased his face. "We use something on our tusks and teeth in the morning and evening. Let me show you."

I followed him to the bathroom with an odd upright

device I hoped was a toilet, since I'd used it as such. A bathtub large enough for three Khols took up a big part of the room, and it had been placed beside the small basin I'd used as a sink. He opened the top of a wooden cabinet and pulled out a jar of something that glowed milky white. I could swear it was made out of crystal. I'd normally be curious about it, because I hadn't seen any evidence of manufacturing here that might create such a thing, but I'd ask him about it and everything else in the morning.

"If you'll be so kind," he whispered, and two crystal tubes with shards jutting up from one end appeared inside the top of the cabinet.

No, they didn't appear like magic. I wasn't going to let my mind dwell on where they'd come from, or I'd start falling apart—again. Clothing appearing on the floor and food emerging from a counter was enough for me for today.

He held out the tube and the jar. "You and Flora can use these to cleanse your teeth."

"Thank you." I took them and lifted my voice. "Flora? Come into the bathroom, please." She still needed help, or she'd eat the toothpaste and pronounce her teeth clean.

"I'll see you in the morning," Khol said softly, his gaze searching mine.

What did he want from me?

Perhaps the water spirit would one day tell me.

KHOL

After I left Nancy in the bathing area with Flora, I heard water running and assumed they were taking a bath. They emerged from my bedroom a while later with damp hair and wearing matching pink nightgowns, courtesy of the water spirit. My needs were small. The spirit must be excited to have others to give gifts to.

Nancy helped Flora settle into her room before returning to my bedroom and shutting the door.

I ached to be with her when I shouldn't. But no matter how many times I reminded myself of the shame I'd felt after Weela was murdered, of the sadness I felt while betraying my friend, I couldn't let go of the feeling that I should pursue Nancy.

It was too soon. There may never be a time for us. And I was going to accept that.

Thankfully, the house spirit expanded the sofa to accommodate my large frame. I slept relatively well, waking as dawn cracked open the world and let light shine through. Birds chirped in the jungle nearby, and the low ripple of the stream made me eager to go for a swim in the pool at the base of the falls.

I sprung up and smiled as the couch resumed its original shape.

"Thank you. That was wonderful," I said, and a splash rang out from the water flowing beneath my snug home. "I have a plan. I have a plan." And I was repeating myself, but oh, well.

Would Nancy help? If not, I'd do it alone.

The plan was for Flora. Such a sweet youngling, so curious and excited. I couldn't wait to see her eyes sparkle with joy once more. While her mother and I might never form anything together, I could make the next few days special for this child. Then, when I left them at the Indigan Clan to begin their new life, I could finally feel proud for having done something to balance what happened.

Flora emerged from her bedroom, yawning while rubbing her eyes. After scooting into my bedroom to use the bathing area, she returned, walking over to stand in front of me, frowning. "Blue man."

"That's me. Blue man, though you can call me Khol. Good morning."

Her head tilted. "Are you my daddy?"

"Oh, no."

Yet I longed for it to be true. What would it be like to claim this child as my own, to show her how to survive in this new world, to help raise her to be a strong, independent person?

Her sigh rang out. "I's want a daddy." She climbed onto the sofa, stretching out her legs, and peered around. "Where's da TV?"

"What's a TV?" I sunk down onto the sofa beside her.

"I wanna watch my shows."

"Could you construct a TV?" I asked the water spirit.

Nothing happened.

"We don't have one," I said. "I'm sorry."

She nodded sadly. "Books? Toys?"

I didn't have any of those either, but I held back the words, fearing her eyes would give way to her sadness and create water like the day before. My clan spirit was infinitely wise. Look at them gifting me with two beings who used water to show their emotions even if I couldn't include them in my life moving forward.

"Would you like to eat?" I asked.

She squinted up at me. "Cereal? I like cereal in da morning."

I rose. "Let me see what I can make in the kitchen." I could cook. I'd done so when I lived with my old clan. But the water spirit loved crafting new dishes, so I let them handle my meals. I walked over to the counter. "Could we have some . . . see-re-elle?"

A bowl full of creamy-colored squares emerged from the counter, along with a small pitcher holding white liquid. I took it over to the table.

"Here you are," I told Flora. "Come sit, and I'll tell you a story while you eat."

"Okay." She slid off the sofa and climbed up into the chair that had to be six times her size. Like last night, it shrunk to accommodate her petite frame.

I added an eating implement, then went to the counter again. "Tea for me, if you please." One of the humans had recently introduced tea to Zuldrux, and it was so tasty that many of the clans had started brewing the herbal liquid to sip in the morning. I particularly enjoyed one of the varieties that had a slightly spicy-sweet flavor.

The water spirit accommodated my wish with a full mug swirling with steam that I carried over to the table.

Flora stared at her see-re-elle but didn't appear to have eaten any.

"Can I get you anything else?" I asked.

"Mommy always pours my milk."

Was that what the white stuff inside the pitcher was called? I lifted it and dumped some of the liquid over the see-re-elle, watching as the squares floated to the top. Such an odd food, but if Flora wanted it, she would have it. Thankfully, the spirit appeared able to fill her needs.

While I sipped my tea, she dug in, scooping up a mix of the liquid and squares, shoveling them into her mouth. She wiggled and hummed while she chewed.

"Tell me a Cwis-mas story?" she asked.

I needed to figure out griss-maas fast. Perhaps Flora could help me, then I could put my plan into place.

"Let's tell a story together. Tell me about . . . griss-maas."

"Cwis-mas," she said, taking another bite. "Der's Santa and stockings and da twee. And Pwesents. I love pwesents."

Presents, I could handle. The water spirit would help. "Who's Santa?"

"He drives da sleigh wit pwesents."

I could do that. "What else?"

"Der's reindeer and a big sack a toys for all da good girls and boys. He wears a red suit."

Was Santa real or was it a made-up story?

"Santa usually comes on Christmas eve," Nancy said, joining us in the dining area. She still wore her pink nightie, and I gaped at her long, slender legs and the way the thin fabric hugged her lush frame. This woman was the prettiest person I'd ever seen.

My heart hollowed out because I couldn't have her or whatever life she might offer.

She paused beside the table, her gaze sliding from Flora's meal to my mug. "I don't suppose you have more of whatever you're drinking?"

"Tea," I said. "Amanda shared how to make it."

"Amanda?" Hope lifted her voice. "Is she one of us?"

"She's from your planet like you, but she's one of us now too. She's mated to Xax of the Ulistar Clan." A wise male would take her to them right away. He wouldn't sit here hoping he could find a way to show Nancy she belonged here. "A storm is coming. The sea will be too rough to cross until after it passes, but we'll travel after that."

She glanced toward the front window. "How big a storm?"

I shrugged. "Not too large, I don't think. We'll weather it fine here. I'll get you some tea." I rose and strode to the counter. "Do you want see-ree-elle also?"

She frowned at Flora's bowl. The youngling kept eating, wiggling and humming in her chair. "Is that what that is?"

"The water spirit made it for her."

"Right." Her lips thinned. The sooner the spirit convinced her of its existence, the better.

I returned to the table with a second cup of tea, plus doo-nuts I requested as an alternative to see-re-elle. Their sweetness had captured me the night before, and I suspected they'd do well for the morning meal. I placed the plateful in the center of the table and dropped back down in my chair, nudging my head toward the other chair and her tea. "Tell me more about Santa, Flora."

Nancy sat and lifted her cup, blowing steam off the top of her tea before taking a tentative sip. Her eyes widened.

"This is delicious. Caffeine? Please tell me there's caffeine in this brew."

Fortunately, Amanda had explained about coo-fee and the burst of caffeine it gave those who drink it.

"Yes," I said, and Nancy's eyes widened. She wiggled in her chair like her youngling daughter and sipped more of her tea. "I can tell you about Santa," she finally said, lowering her mug to the table.

She shared a tale about a jolly male who dressed in bright red clothing with white trim. He visited younglings all over her world on one night alone to deliver presents. The Earth village the women came from must be small to make such a thing possible.

I wasn't exactly sure what reindeer were, but I'd hunted fleet-footed creatures in the jungle that sounded similar.

"Do you eat reindeer?" I asked once the Santa tale was finished. "I could hunt for one later, and we could eat the creature's meat tonight. Our gods only provide vegetables, grains, and fruit, never meat."

Flora's lower lip trembled, and she gave way to her clan-appropriate water emotion, allowing it to trickle down her cheeks. "Are we gonna eat Woo-dolph?"

"No," I cried, shooting Khol a sharp look. "We would never eat Santa's reindeer."

Thankfully, Flora believed me and stopped crying. She shoved her nearly finished bowl of cereal away and slid off her chair. "I's done. No TV. No toys. No books. What am I gonna do, Mommy?"

She sounded so dejected that I left my chair and gave her a hug. "We'll find something that'll be just as fun." I had no idea what it might be.

Khol was a bachelor Zuldruxian, and he lived alone here on this island. I doubted he had many visitors, let alone those with children. Why would he keep toys around?

"I'll finish my tea, and we can sit on the sofa," I said. "I'll tell you a bunch of stories." It was a good thing I was creative, but I suspected story time was going to be the only entertainment I could offer.

Where would she go to school? If I had books, I could teach her, but I didn't see one in sight.

This place didn't appear to offer dental care, a hospital or doctor's office, let alone a supermarket. I wasn't like my ancestors who could survive on the windy plains, living inside a sod house, eating only what I could grow or catch in the wild.

Flora climbed onto the sofa and stretched out her legs. She stared around. "I wanna have fun, Mommy. Make it fun!"

"She's used to going to daycare," I told Khol, explaining what that was. "There, she can play with her friends. They have lots of toys and books. Janet sits them down a couple times during the day to teach them their ABCs and how to write their name. Flora's smart. She can read some of the simpler picture books already, though that could be because she's memorized them. I've read to her every night since she was little."

"I have some ideas for her," he said, his lips curling up in a sweet smile. He really was gorgeous, if in an alien way. His muscles were drool-worthy, and he was so tall and broad. I suspected if he held me, I'd feel like nothing could ever harm me. If this was just me, I'd be sorely tempted to think of myself as his new mate and see where the idea took me.

But I had my daughter with me, and her needs had to come first. I'd been careful when I dated, never introducing her to any of the guys. Until one wanted us both equally, I didn't want her to get attached to someone only to have us break up and him disappear from her life.

My heart couldn't take something like that either, so I'd rarely gone out with anyone. Why risk being hurt again?

"Could you give Flora some toys like she might have in her home village?" Khol asked.

"Oh, I don't have anything like that." I frowned. He'd seen me arrive, the pod we'd flown in splashing into the water. It sank quickly. Even if I'd brought things for us, they'd be resting at the bottom of the sea.

"Very good," he said, his smile growing wider. "You're amazing."

I followed his gaze to Flora, who squealed and slid off the couch. A wooden box I would swear hadn't been there a moment ago now sat on the table in front of the sofa.

Flora reached inside and pulled out a pile of books, dropping them onto the cushions. "Magic, Mommy." She added a bunch of toys and even a blankie like the one she'd carried everywhere inside her princess backpack. Who knew where that had gone when the robocops took us?

Flora hugged the blanket to her chest before laying it on the couch. After climbing up beside the good-sized pile of "magic," she tugged a book onto her lap and started to flip through it, exclaiming about the pictures.

"This isn't possible," I said, my voice shaky.

"My clan water spirit is quite kind. They were so welcoming when my boat washed up onto this shore that I knew this was where I belonged. I hope . . ." His soft gaze met mine, and he swallowed. "I hope you'll feel at home here too, if only for the short time you'll be with me."

"I don't understand." Shock filled my voice. "I mean, I saw clothing appear from the floor last night, plus the dirty dishes somehow slip down into the kitchen counter." I flicked my hand to the perfect-appearing donuts I hadn't yet dared try. "My daughter's calling this magic."

"This shows the spirit's kindness."

"It doesn't make sense," I said shrilly. Last night, when I couldn't find a way to turn on the water in the tub, I'd grumbled something about it under my breath. Water started gushing, the perfect temperature for a bath. Flora and I had bathed together, and I'd tried not to notice how the tub emptied after we'd stepped out—all on its own. "There's no such thing as water spirits performing magic."

"Yet they do things for us," he said softly. "I think they're an alien lifeform much like you. Me, too, I suppose, though I was born on this planet. They adore being kind, and all they ask in return is that we thank them. Honestly, we got used to it quickly. How could we not when they would give us clothing or food or the toys Flora's playing with at our request?"

It was much easier to accept this was some kind of symbiotic alien species than a god or a spirit. How could I complain when an alien lifeform was eager to cook my meals, wash my clothing, and give my precious daughter enough toys to keep her occupied for hours?

My heart rate slowed, and I told my mind to stop racing. This would work out—somehow. With or without Khol.

Did I dare trust his water spirit to make our lives better?

It was the season of hope and joy, and maybe, just maybe, I should let some of it into my heart and see what happened.

Trust bloomed inside me, for Khol and this precarious situation, and I was going to cling to it for now. He wasn't asking me for anything other than my company, I supposed.

He mentioned a storm was coming, that he'd take me to the other women after it ended. They'd explain everything, and then I could start figuring out what I wanted to do with my life.

As for Khol . . . He was thoughtful and treating us better than most would even if they didn't think I was their "fated mate," but I couldn't let myself start over with someone new.

Could I?

There was no need to decide now. I'd just met him. Settling into a new life on this planet needed to be my only goal.

With renewed purpose, I walked over to the table, where I lifted a donut and took a big bite, savoring how perfectly it matched the flavor of donuts back home.

Home?

I'd always felt that home was where the heart is.

Was there a place for my heart to bloom here on Zuldrux?

CHAPTER 12
KHOL

I was grateful when the panic left Nancy's eyes. Even more grateful that the spirit knew what Flora needed to make her happy.

"I have a plan," I said softly as Nancy sat and finished her doo-nut. I took one from the pile and ate it in one bite, chewing and swallowing before eyeing the others. What other interesting food could Nancy introduce to Zuldrux? I suspected my friends would enjoy what I'd tasted so far.

"You mentioned a plan that last night," Nancy said, her hand dropping to lay on mine sitting on the table. She was so much tinier than me and seeing our hands touching only reinforced it. If I could dismiss my past and look toward the future, I might be willing to accept the water spirit's plan. That would mean Nancy was my new mate, someone who would stand by my side and make my life feel complete.

Yet she was so much smaller than me. I'd give anything not to hurt her.

I was of average size for a Zuldruxian, but I was bigger than her all over. Even if we somehow decided to trust in the water spirit's plan, were intimate relations possible between us?

Aizor and Vanessa were in love and clearly together in every way. It was the same with Nevarn and Kerry, plus Amanda and Xax.

Intimacy was physically possible between our two species.

I couldn't quite fathom something like this. Not our bodies joining, though I hadn't yet tried something like that, but the thought of no longer being alone.

But my cock . . .

The spirits wouldn't send her to me if it . . . wouldn't fit, so I wasn't going to worry about that.

I reminded myself that she and I would not be mating. Soon the storm would pass, and I'd take her to the Indigan Clan, where she'd settle. Within no time, the gods would give her a new mate, and she'd be with him.

Never me.

"What's your plan?" she asked, taking another doo-nut and biting into it.

I leaned close to her, keeping my voice low. "I want to give Flora the griss-maas she longs for, but I'll need help."

Her frown smoothed. "Aw, that's very sweet of you."

Sweet wasn't handsome or a word a female might use if she was eager to mate with a male, but I'd claim it for now.

I could tell myself I didn't deserve more, but my heart refused to listen. It kept flipping over whenever she was near and longing.

So much longing . . .

I needed to focus on my plan and forget about being with her.

I continued to speak in a soft tone so Flora wouldn't overhear. "We need a twee and—"

Nancy's laugh burst out, low and husky and incredibly attractive. My cocks took notice, and the larger one started shifting beneath my pants. I told it to behave.

"Tree," she emphasized. "Though I love how you pronounce it." Her gaze shot to her daughter who continued to look through the book on her lap. "Flora was going to speech therapy. I'll have to continue that here. She's still learning how to pronounce her words. She's only four-years-old, and as she grows older, language will come easier to her."

"Ah." I'd wondered how old she was. "She's very tiny." So much smaller than a Zuldruxian at that age. And smart. I could see this already.

Flora was reciting a story that may or may not be related to the book she scrolled through. I'd only seen a few books before, thick tomes the elders sometimes referred to for how to settle disputes or interact with distant clans. They'd seemed dull and dry to me, but I suspected Flora's books were anything but. I would study them later.

"She's average sized for her age," Nancy said. "But I suspect all humans would appear small to a Zuldruxian. Are your women as large as your males?"

"Most. They're warriors as well, and quite muscular. They have four breasts." My gaze dropped to her two. They were smooth and round and full, and I ached to discover what they felt like. "Zuldruxian females nurse their young from tubes that project below their relatively flat breasts after a youngling is born."

Nancy's frown returned. "That's very interesting. We have nipples."

"What are nipples?"

Color filled her face, making her even prettier. "I think that's something we can discuss later."

"Perhaps you can show them to me, and I'll better understand."

Her face got even darker. "Right." She took a sip of her tea and returned the mug to the table. "Back to Christmas."

"Yes, tell me about your traditions, because I want to bring them into my home here on Zuldrux."

She explained about the tree, stockings—whatever those were—the meal, and presents, and how they celebrated all while making sure they held hope and joy in their hearts.

It sounded complicated to me, but I was intrigued enough to give this time of joy a chance. Joy had not been part of my life for a very long time.

"Some believe in Christmas miracles," she said.

"What's a miracle?"

"Something special that happens that almost feels like magic or as if the fates are intervening."

I did not deserve a griss-maas miracle. I'd had my chance, and it was gone forever.

"We can do this," I said, determined to make this good for Flora and Nancy. "When should we hold our griss-maas?"

"It was a few days away when we were kidnapped from Earth. I have no idea what the date is here."

"We don't have anything called dates. One day passes into the next. Certain areas of Zuldrux see different seasons, some cold and others very hot. Here on my island, one day is much like the next. The only difference between them is whether it rains or not."

"This looks like the tropical islands I read about on Earth, but I'm sure we can make Christmas work anywhere. It's more about the feeling in your heart than tangible things, though that's what Flora's focusing on now."

"Shall we hold it in three days time, then?" That gave me time to work on my plan.

"That would be amazing. Thank you." She squeezed my hand still on the table.

"You're welcome."

We weren't holding hands, but I'd been reluctant to draw away after she made the initial contact.

Despite telling myself I wasn't worthy of a new mate, that I'd had my chance, and it ended, I was beginning to crave this woman in a way unlike any other.

If I wasn't careful, my eyes would start leaking water of sadness like a human's did, and I didn't want to cause Flora or Nancy further distress.

My heart warmed whenever I looked Nancy's way, and I was filled with such intense longing that I worried it would eat through me and tumble out the other side.

"Let's cut a tree," I announced to distract myself.

Flora squealed and tossed aside her book. She slid off the sofa and raced over to stand in front of me. "Can we, Daddy? Can we?"

"Khol isn't your daddy," Nancy rushed to say. Her cheeks had turned pink, and she shot me a look I couldn't quite interpret. "I'm terribly sorry," she told me. "She and I have talked about this. She knows she has a birth father but that he's not part of our lives."

"I want a daddy, Mommy," Flora said, her lips quivering and water filling her eyes. "Khol can be my daddy."

I left my chair and stooped down in front of her. "I'll always be your friend, little one. Trust in that." Yet once I left her with the Indigan Clan, someone else would woo Nancy. They'd adore Flora as much as me, and if he and Nancy mated, Flora would call him daddy.

My heart was breaking, and I'd only known Flora and

Nancy for a short time. How could the gods be so cruel as to send me two special people like them only to make me give them away?

I didn't deserve love and happiness, not when it was stolen from Weela.

Yet my heart ached to give this a try.

No, I couldn't. I'd stick to my plan to give them a special griss-maas, and once the storm was over, I'd take them to the mainland.

Then I'd find a way to tell them goodbye.

"What kind of tree should we get?" I asked, truly not knowing, but also wanting to distract myself from my thoughts. My heart also ached for this youngling to call me her father. Was I foolish to let that feeling grow inside me? Probably, but I couldn't seem to help it.

"A green one," Flora said pertly. "Bushy and wit needles."

"That you suck up."

Nancy blinked at me. "We don't suck on the tree>"

"I, um . . ." I must've misheard her the evening before." I frowned. "We don't have green trees here on my island or anywhere else, actually. Zuldrux vegetation is purple."

"Purple will be gorgeous with red and white decorations." Nancy clapped her hands. "Let's walk around and pick out a tree. We can bring it inside and see if the water spirit will help us make decorations." From her frown, I could tell she remained skeptical, but who wouldn't be? It didn't sound as if her people worshipped anything like the beings who'd landed on Zuldrux long ago.

We left the house and walked out into the middle of the meadow.

"How we gonna cut da twee?" Flora asked, peering

around at the jungle full of enormous trees, vines, and lush, thorny vegetation.

"Let me grab my tool." I jogged to the smaller building where I kept my supplies and emerged with a saw. I'd cut all the trees to build my house, and the water spirit had helped turn the thick tree trunks into boards for my building.

We walked into the jungle, Nancy holding Flora's hand.

"Where's the Cwis-mas trees, Mommy?" Flora asked, her head tilted back and a frown on her face. "Dees aren't right."

"We use evergreens back home," Nancy said. "They're dark green and they have needles rather than leaves."

Needles that she did *not* suck up.

I paused to think of the various vegetation on my island. "Our trees are purple. That can't be changed, but . . ." Ah, yes. "Follow me."

I led them down a winding trail that snaked toward the middle of the island.

"I's tired a walking, Mommy," Flora said.

"Hold on." Nancy glanced my way.

When she started to lift Flora, I strode over and handed her my saw. "Can you hold this for me?"

"Oh, um, sure." She frowned down at it, and it was comically large in her hands.

"It's not too heavy?"

The strips of hair above her eyes lifted. "I've carried my daughter around her entire life."

"Which I'll do for you now." I lifted Flora, and she squealed with excitement. When I sat her on my shoulder and held her in place, she latched onto my hair.

"Yay," she cried out. "We's goin' for a ride." She rocked

forward, kicking her heels against my chest. "Fast. Go fast, Khol."

My low laugh rang out. "Do you want me to run, youngling?"

"What's a yung-ling?" she asked, her cute face scrunching.

"You, little one. You're a youngling."

"I's a yung-ling," she cried, rocking faster. "We's gonna run through da jungle. Yay."

"We're going to walk," I told Nancy quietly.

Nancy bit down on her lower lip. "Are you sure? I don't mind carrying her."

"She's a pleasure to hold."

Taking the saw in my other hand, I started walking.

Nancy strode along beside me. "It's lovely here. So warm and tropical."

"What's your climate like where you came from?"

She talked about their cold winters and warm summers, how the in between seasons were more moderate.

"I can't imagine snot," I said.

She paused on the trail, blinking up at me before her laughter trilled out. "I'm not making fun of you. Snow. Not snot, though when they throw sand and dirt on it to keep people from slipping, it does resemble snot."

"Snot," Flora said, wiggling on my shoulder. "Snot!"

"We'll find trees straight ahead," I said with a laugh, continuing walking.

We chuckled as we strode out into a big clearing full of new growth trees. They didn't bear needles, and I wasn't sure why anyone would get excited about trees covered with tiny sharp objects, but they might do for our holiday.

Zuldruxians held celebrations for various reasons, but

we didn't have anything like griss-maas. I was already as excited about this as Flora.

How could I make the rest of my plan work? Tonight, after they went to bed, I'd think about ways I could do this for them.

I stopped beside one of the trees, unsure how big they'd want or how I'd keep it alive inside my house. "What about this one?"

Nancy walked around the tree, frowning.

Flora continued bucking, calling out for me to go faster. I scooped her up off my shoulder and gently placed her on her feet, keeping a hold of her hand.

"As you said, it's purple," Nancy said. "The branches are kind of thick and it doesn't have many leaves."

Her frown wasn't going away.

We could look for other trees. It didn't have to be this one. In fact—

"But I love it," Nancy said, smiling up at me. "It'll be perfect."

Khol cut the tree and hefted it, slinging it over his shoulder.

It looked nothing like evergreens on Earth, but it was pretty in its own unique, alien way. Purple, but so was all the vegetation on this planet. I was rapidly getting used to the color.

And to the warm feelings Khol kept generating inside me, feelings I wasn't sure I dared trust. It was hard to put yourself out there to someone, to pretty much hand them your heart. Richard hurt me.

But Khol wasn't Richard.

No, he was a nice guy who was still mourning his lost love.

As we walked back to his house with him carrying both Flora and the tree and me hefting the saw, I watched the way he teased my daughter and how happily she responded to him. He really was an amazing person, and he'd make someone the perfect mate.

Me?

I could've wound up in a worse place than a tropical

island with a blue-skinned alien who seemed determined to give my daughter and me joy.

Yet he was going to take us to another clan and leave us.

A silly voice inside me suggested he wouldn't want to leave us if I started showing him he mattered, that he was worthy of love.

We were two lost hearts. Could we nudge our hurt aside to find something new together?

It was too soon to decide. I had days. Weeks. Years if I wanted. Just because he was going to take us somewhere and leave us, that didn't mean I had to accept that plan. I could tell him Flora and I wanted to join his clan, that I wanted to see what might come of this spirit-induced mating.

My heart skipped at the thought of doing something like that. It was a big risk for someone who'd told herself she would never try again. But life was too short to waste it by letting one bad experience cloud the rest of my future.

Something wonderful could be waiting for me; I just had to let it into my heart.

We arrived at his house and, after tilting the tree against the front wall beside the door, he carefully placed Flora on the ground. Her cheeks were pink, and her eyes shone with excitement. I couldn't remember the last time she'd been this happy just running around in the woods and doing something as simple as cutting a tree.

"We need ta get it inside," Flora exclaimed, bustling over to the door and pushing it open.

"Do you have a bucket or something to put the trunk in?" I asked.

He thought about it for a moment before his face cleared. "I know exactly what we need." Hefting the tree, he strode inside the house. He placed the tree on the floor in front of the sofa and returned to the front door. "I'll be right back."

As he left, I turned to Flora. "We need to start making ornaments."

"Yay," she said, hopping over to stand in front of me. "Can we paint and use dough?"

Dough would work if I could find the right ingredients. I'd made a dough with salt, flour, and water in the past.

Water spirit . . .

"Let's go see if the local alien can give us what we need," I said, taking Flora's hand and striding over to stand in front of the counter.

I'd never spoken to a water spirit before, but I'd chatted quite a bit with the resident alien, Khol. No harm in trying, right?

I laid my hand on the counter and lifted my voice. "Um, water . . . err, Taikeen Clan spirit? Flora and I want to make ornaments, but we need specific ingredients. Water—"

An empty bowl oozed up from the counter along with a cup of water. Maybe this would work.

After sending Flora a smile, which she returned, hopping in place, I turned back to the counter. "I also need salt. The ocean's salty, but I need only the salt, not salty water."

A bowl of white crystals appeared. I hesitated a second before licking my finger and dipping it into the crystals, tentatively tasting it. Yup, it tasted just like the stuff back on Earth.

"Yummy, Mommy?" Flora asked, tilting her head to watch me.

"Nope. Thank you, Taikeen . . . err, spirit."

The counter glowed, and I sucked in a breath, taking a

step backward. Khol had said his house spirit enjoyed praise. Was that all it took to get what I needed?

"And flour. I'd love a five-pound bag of that if you can . . . create it for me."

Nothing new appeared on the counter. What would make a good substitution for flour? We weren't baking with it, though I'd wondered if I could make cookies over the next few days.

"Where da fwower?" Flora asked. "We need fwower."

"Flour." I drew out the word, waiting while she repeated it for me.

When she'd gotten it right, I ruffled her hair.

"Spirit of the Taikeen Clan?" I asked. "Flour is made from ground grains and it's white and powdery. Look in your computer, if you have anything like that, and you'll find a description. We'd love some food-grade flour, because we're going to make cookies soon too."

"Yes, cookies," Flora squealed. "Lots and lots of cookies."

We waited while the world ticked by, and just when I was beginning to give up hope, a larger bowl with what looked like flour appeared on the counter.

"Yay," Flora cried out. "We got it."

"We sure did, sweetie." Maybe. I tasted it, though I wasn't sure I'd ever eaten plain flour before, and it seemed like what I was used to back on Earth.

Khol returned with a small pail full of water. While Flora and I mixed our dough, he placed the tree trunk in the pail and secured the top to the wall with a few pieces of vine, keeping it standing upright. After, he stood back to admire it. "It's . . . nice."

"It's going to be gorgeous," I said. "Come help us make

some ornaments. I don't suppose you have an oven, do you?"

"I do."

"Really? What do you bake?"

"So far, only meatloaf."

A married meal from Earth? That's what I once heard someone call it, like it was a dish every bride made not long after the honeymoon was over. Like it was a staple in everyone's marriage. Or, on Zuldrux, a bachelor's meal, I supposed. "Where did you hear about meatloaf?" Actually, there was no reason aliens wouldn't have discovered how to make it themselves. He said he ate meat.

"Vanessa taught me."

My breath caught. "One of the other women cooks?"

"Yes." He flashed me a smile that made my heart flip over. "She loves to bake, and her mate, Aizor, built her an oven." I loved seeing the excitement in his eyes as he described how he'd collected the right stones here on the island and mixed mortar to hold them together. How he'd measured his oven to make sure it was big enough to hold the very flat rocks he used for cookie sheets, and how he selected exactly the right wood to bake with, wood that didn't generate lots of smoke unless he wanted to give his meat that yummy flavor. How he used ground meat from creatures he trapped on the island.

"When I visited the Indigan Clan after the gathering," he said, "Vanessa showed her oven to me, and I studied how Aizor made it. It wasn't hard to recreate it here. As I said, my clan spirit doesn't provide meat. I enjoy the fish I catch and the meat from small creatures I trap in the jungle, but in the past, I'd fry or cook the meat over a fire on a stick. Being able to cook something slower and with steady heat

is a joy. I also cook roasts, and I bake my fish with season-
ings I collect near the stream."

"This sounds amazing." I peered around. "Where's your
oven?"

"Since I fuel it with wood, I built it behind my house."

"Could you fire it up?"

His gaze fell on the dough we'd just finished kneading.
"When would you like to have the oven ready?"

"In a few hours. We still have to finish rolling and
cutting our ornaments, but they should be ready for baking
by then."

Ornaments were on the agenda for today.

Tomorrow, I was going to bake some cookies.

CHAPTER 14

KHOL

I collected wood and got everything ready to bake our ornaments, though I wasn't exactly sure what they were.

Because the wind kept gusting, heralding the coming storm, I erected a shade to protect my oven and help keep the flame even. Vanessa made it very clear that the heat level—she called it temp-a-toor had to be steady or the food would bake too much on one side and not enough on the other.

Back inside, I paused to watch Nancy and Flora. Flora stood on a chair at the counter beside Nancy, and they were busy working with their dough. The only dough I knew of was the one Vanessa used to make pee-za, and it was delicious. But surely pee-za dough wasn't used to make items to hang on the tree. Or maybe we'd eat them off the tree later. That could be what she'd meant when she brought up sucking up needles.

"Can I help?" I asked, joining them.

Nancy sent me a sweet smile. "Sure."

Her smile shouldn't make me ache to pick her up and

kiss her, but it did. It also shouldn't make me want to take her to my bedroom, kick the door shut, and lay her on the blankets where I could devour every bit of her. But it did.

I was falling for Nancy, just as the gods intended, and I couldn't seem to hold myself back.

Was there hope for a male who'd lost his way and was struggling to find a new path into the future?

I'd focus on my goal to give Flora the best griss-maas ever and see what happened after I took her to the mainland. If Nancy wanted to remain with the Indigan Clan, I'd walk away from her with my head high and acceptance in my heart.

And if she wanted to return to the island with me?

I wasn't going to let myself dream of anything like that.

We rolled the dough into a thin sheet and used a blade to cut shapes. Under Nancy's direction, we added holes at the top of each and laid them out on the very flat rock I used to bake my roasts.

When we'd used up all the dough, we stared at our creations. We'd made five-pointed designs Flora called stars, though the stars in the sky didn't look anything like these. Designs that were supposed to resemble trees. Balls, though I didn't know why we'd be eager to hang a replica of a toy on the tree. Flora also made what she called kee-tees, though Nancy pointed out she'd only made their heads.

A kee-tee looked a bit like a grundar. Nevarn's new mate, Kerry, had tamed a grundar, and it lived inside their tree home with them, even sleeping on their bed at night. I wasn't sure I wanted a grundar lying on my bed with me, but perhaps I would if I got to know the grundar first.

Nancy had crafted stock-ings, and she had to explain what they were. I mostly walked barefoot, though many Zuldruxians wore shoes or boots—without stock-ings.

Should I ask our god to make some for us? They sounded like something I might enjoy wearing when it got cold at night.

I went out to check my oven, finding it nearly ready to bake our ornaments. The wind kept gusting, and I paused on my way back to my house, peering at the sky. It may be nothing . . .

But I'd climb the tallest tree nearby periodically to keep an eye on the horizon. Wind like this sometimes heralded a large storm, and if one like that was coming, I needed to be prepared.

Inside, I lifted the thin slab of rock and Nancy and Flora followed me back outside, Flora dancing and singing about the reindeer named Woo-dolf. Such a cute song. She'd recited the words to me inside as we cut our shapes, and the song didn't take long to learn. Because it was fun, I sang it along with her.

Nancy kept smiling, and hope bloomed in my heart when it shouldn't.

I enjoyed my isolated island life, but I'd be dishonest if I didn't admit that I was lonely.

A male could be complete on his own.

But a mate by his side could make him feel even better.

CHAPTER 15
NANCY

Our ornaments came out of the oven looking great, and we made plans to craft something similar to paint the next day while our cookies baked in Khol's amazing oven.

While the wind gusted our cozy house, we shared dinner and sat in the living area afterward, talking. Flora played, and I realized this place was beginning to feel like home.

That night, as I slept in Khol's bed, I drank in his light, fresh scent permeating the blankets that was both comforting and vaguely arousing. I woke up twice in the middle of steamy dreams about him, and I wasn't sure what to do about it, if anything.

He still loved his lost mate, and there wasn't any room for me in a bed like that.

For the first time in I didn't know how long, I woke the next morning feeling eager for the day to get started. I loved my daughter. I'd never once considered not keeping her after I discovered I was pregnant. But it was hard being a single parent. Flora was a sweetie, but so many times, especially during late-night feedings or when she was cranky, I would've loved to have a shoulder to lean on, someone to help me laugh through the tough times while smiling and savoring the best.

There were only two days left until our improvised Christmas, though the date was fluid since the Zuldruxians only observed seasons. But it was something to look forward to.

I slid out of bed and bathed, dressing in the fresh sundress the house provided.

We had breakfast together and returned everything to the counter.

Once it was clear, I thought about what we needed for today's projects.

"Paint," I said. "I think there's a way to make it, and we can look for plants to dye it in various colors." I described paintbrushes to Khol, and he nodded slowly.

"I know something that will work." He left to collect plants plus construct our paintbrushes.

I stared at the empty counter while Flora played with her toys in the living room.

Could I try salt and flour again? If I made it runny, it might work. There was no harm in trying.

"Um, house spirit?" I asked, peering up at the ceiling. "Could I have five or six small bowls we can use to make various colors of paint?"

Six tiny bowls appeared on the counter.

"Thank you. This looks wonderful." This wasn't much different from talking to my phone or Alexa except this smart house came with more benefits. If only my phone could've cooked dinner or cleaned the house when I was worn out after coming home with my daughter from the hospital. My mom was excited about having a grandchild, but she lived far away, and she worked two jobs to make ends meet. It was too expensive to travel often. We chatted on the phone, and I sent lots of pictures, but the economy kept us apart. I'd handled everything alone for much too long. It was nice having Khol here to help with Flora and to talk with. What would it be like to have a partner like him around all the time?

It was silly to think of something like that. We would only be here for a few days before we'd leave for the mainland. Once he'd brought us to the Indigan Clan, he'd turn and leave and I might never see him again. My heart felt bruised against my ribs at the thought, but I couldn't see what I could do about it.

My mom would be worried about me and Flora. I could only imagine the horror she must be experiencing now. Someone would call her when I didn't show up at work; I'd named her as my next of kin in the paperwork I'd filled out when I was hired. Janet would tell her I'd picked up Flora after daycare, but she would've been busy with the kids inside and I doubt she would've seen the robocops take us. Would her neighbors? Probably not at that time of day; most people were still at work. My poor mom wouldn't know what happened to us.

"I don't suppose you could send word to my mom that I'm okay," I said softly. "Truly, it was mean of you guys to steal us without at least giving us a chance to tell our family and friends goodbye."

The counter glowed before dimming, but I had no idea if that meant the water spirit would send word to Earth or not. It wasn't like this god could hop into a ship and travel there to tell her in person.

My mom would mourn, and the worst part about it was

that she'd think something horrible happened to me and Flora.

I swallowed back my tears. They'd do me no good here.

And I started mixing the base for our paint.

Khol returned and held up a handful of sticks with tiny brushes tied to the ends.

"When you described your paintbrush, I thought of this plant. I think it'll work well." He laid a big clump of various leaves and flowers on the counter. Plenty of colors.

"We could boil them until the water's almost absorbed," I said.

Tiny pans appeared on the counter, and I tore up the vegetation, dropping each into their own pan, adding a bit of water.

"How do we cook things?" I asked, peering around.

"Like this." Khol placed all the tiny pans on a separate, narrow counter and hummed. The counter started warming until it glowed with heat. The water boiled, and a pungent smell filled the air.

"Stinky," Flora said, scrunching her face. She stood, leaning her belly against the back of the sofa.

"Paint is coming right up," I said brightly. "Since it's already afternoon, I think we should hold off making our cookies until tomorrow."

"Cookies," Flora cried, hopping on the sofa.

"Down before you fall, sweetie," I said, and she plunked back onto her butt and started reading again.

"Would you like to swim in the pool below the falls this afternoon?" Khol asked.

"Swim," Flora shouted. "Wanna swim, Mommy."

I sent him a smile. "I'd love to. Hey, smart house, we'll need bathing suits."

Brightly colored fabric appeared on the counter.

I was beginning to enjoy life here on Zuldrux.

Once the water had boiled off, I drizzled the liquid into each of my improvised paint bowls, giving each a solid stir.

They looked amazing. Now to try them out.

We grabbed brushes and started painting our ornaments.

I needed to figure out presents. Could I ask the house god to help with that? It felt like cheating, like maybe I should be making them myself like people did ages ago on Earth. But asking the house spirit to help wasn't much different from going to the store and buying toys, then wrapping them in pretty paper.

"Beautiful," Khol said from beside me, pointing to the ball-shaped ornament I'd decorated with swirls and dots. The paint worked great, and they were going to look fantastic on the tree.

"Your trees are amazing," I said. He'd painted most of them purple, but he'd decorated two in green in honor of the trees back on Earth. He'd shaped dough into something like the pink no-kitties we saw here when we first arrived, to Flora's amazement, plus some that looked like flowers.

"Thank you."

"All they need to do now is dry, and then we can hang them on the tree. We'll need to find thin vines for the holes."

"I know where I can get some." His gaze slanted my way, and for one instant, I saw stark need there before his face smoothed into a neutral mask. Did he like me more than I'd suspected? Stating his spirit had decided we were mates was one thing. Falling in love with each other was another.

The thought of giving my heart to someone new was scary. But Khol was a big sweetie. It would be easy to adore him, to love him.

It was getting harder and harder to hold myself back.

"Would you like to swim now?" he asked after the water spirit cleaned everything up. I could get used to this. Truly.

"Swim," Flora exclaimed, hopping on her chair.

He scooped her up and placed her on her feet, stroking her hair while she gazed up at him with complete adoration. "You need to take your princess gown off or it'll get wet."

"Need my baby-soup," she crowed, scooping the bathing suit up off the back of the sofa and racing to her room.

"I should get changed too," I said.

He nodded, his gaze drifting down my body, heavy enough to feel like a caress. Something was changing between us, and despite my mind shouting danger, I liked it.

It would be very easy to fall hard and fast for Khol.

"Thank you for being kind to Flora," I said. "I know she can be demanding at times. Fussy. But she's got a tender heart."

"She's amazing," he gushed. "So smart. Thoughtful. And she makes me laugh."

I loved that the things he spoke about were inside her and not solely external. Too many people talked about her pretty hair and eyes. Her chirpy voice that made you smile. Khol saw the person inside the lovely package.

Did he also see inside me?

"What happened to her father?" he asked.

I'd wondered when he might get to that. He must've been curious. I hadn't mentioned my ex-boyfriend in conversation other than when she was trying to call Khol daddy. That implied she didn't have one in her life.

"It was a quick thing. I thought I was in love with him, but he was just using me." I cringed, thinking about when he'd laughed at me for believing he loved me, when he turned and strode from my life as if I didn't matter. "We weren't together long. He didn't want a child. He didn't want me."

Khol growled. "What?" he barked.

I winced, though not from his raised voice. "This is embarrassing to talk about."

He held my shoulders. "You're amazing. You're not only lovely but you also have a kind heart. I see how you care for everyone, even me, though we only met a few days ago. You're generous and sweet, and I want to rip this male apart for hurting you, for not loving you."

"Thank you." I tried not to gush because his words warmed me straight through. He didn't mean them, of course, not in more than a friendship way. "Richard walked out of our lives right after I told him I was pregnant. He sent money every month, for a little while, that is. I thank him for what he did give, because it's hard to raise a child alone. But he wanted no part in my or Flora's life. That hurt."

He drew me into his arms and held me like a friend would.

But a fire was smoldering inside me. I was attracted to my ex. I'd wanted him physically and emotionally, but it now seemed like the feelings I'd had for him only scratched the surface of my true potential.

And I sensed the feelings growing inside me for Khol would dive much deeper, all the way to the bottom where they'd bloom and turn into something wonderful if I let them.

Let them?

I had no more control over this than I did with Richard.

Khol still loved Weela. He'd never love me. I needed to accept that. Symbols on our skin wouldn't change that.

Yet I couldn't stop hoping for something with this special guy.

I didn't quite know why I did it, but a wild and unrestrained Nancy took over. I tipped my head back, looking up at him. He was so much taller than me, at least seven feet. And broad. Bulging with muscles. His arms around me made me feel cherished and loved.

Because I wouldn't be able to reach, even if I stood on my toes, I curled my finger toward him.

He lowered his head, his gaze locked on mine.

And I kissed him.

KHOL

Kissing Nancy was like reaching up into the sky during a storm and grabbing onto lightning.

Heat roared through me, centering in my heart. It dove down to smolder in my groin. My cocks shifted, as eager as me to claim this woman as my own.

Her mouth . . . So sweet and tender and with a touch of innocence that drove me out of my mind. I lifted her and gently placed her on the counter, nudging her legs apart to step between them.

I'd give almost anything to be alone with Nancy right now, to peel off her clothing and touch her. To welcome her into my life forever.

Wait. No. I wasn't dreaming of anything like that. Or was I?

Hope was a furious thing, slashing its way through me, and if I could just grab onto it, I sensed something wonderful might happen.

I let it slide away and lifted my head to watch her face, girding myself for the regret I was sure I'd find there. She'd initiated our kiss, but it must've been driven by curiosity.

Regret didn't come. She smiled up at me. "I hope that was okay."

I'd heard the other women use this word, oh-kay, and after time, I finally determined what it meant.

"It was more than oh-kay," I rasped, stroking her cheeks with my big hands. I was huge compared to this tiny female. If I wasn't careful, I'd snap her in two. "I hope it was oh-kay for you."

Damn hope. It kept surging up inside me, driving my actions.

My heart . . .

Oh, my poor, poor heart that was feeling so many amazing things for Nancy.

"I like kissing you, Khol. I thought I'd feel your tusks, but I didn't. Not much, that is. They're firm but they just rested there. Your lips, however . . ."

"My lips?" I asked.

"They . . ." She sucked in a breath and released it. "I liked them very much. Liked kissing you."

"Then we should do it again."

Why had I said that? I waited for her to reject me now, because surely, she would.

Instead, her smile widened, and mine joined in. I felt like I could scale the tallest mountain with one leap. Fly through the sky without wings. And right everything in my sad, lonely world.

"We goin' swimming?" Flora chirped from beside me. "Why Mommy on da counter?"

"Yes, we're going swimming, sweetie," Nancy said. She shot me a smile that made my blood boil before nudging me to step backward. "I was looking at something," she added. "But yes, we're going swimming." After sliding off the counter, she sashayed over to the sofa to grab the outfit the god had provided for swimming. It didn't appear to be much, just a few wisps of cloth.

If her kiss made my blood boil, I could only imagine the heat that would charge through me if I saw her wearing only bits of fabric.

"What will you wear to swim, Khol?" she asked, pausing in the entrance to my bedroom. My bed. My woman if I let her inside my heart and she wanted the same.

If only I dared claim the life she might be offering.

"I don't wear anything to swim," I said.

Her gaze fell on Flora. "You might need to with little eyes about."

"Dats me," Flora said with a nod. "Little eyes."

My grin couldn't get any wider, could it?

"I could wear a loincloth," I said.

"That might be wise. You don't want to give me too much of a view, now do you?" With that, Nancy sauntered into my bedroom.

Maybe I did want to give her a view.

Fire surged through me, and it was all I could do not to succumb to the flames.

What would she think if she saw me completely naked?

CHAPTER 17

NANCY

Things were going . . . Well, I wasn't sure where they were going between Khol and I, but I liked it. His kiss was amazing, his lips were soft yet held a hint of demand that swirled through me like the finest wine on a hot summer day.

It wouldn't be hard to crave this guy unlike any other.

Did I dare trust my heart to someone who still mourned his lost love?

Fortunately, I didn't have to think about it now. We'd only kissed. It wasn't like we'd gone to bed together or declared our feelings.

This afternoon was for swimming and tomorrow, we'd do some more decorating and make cookies. With only a few days left until Christmas, there was enough to do to keep me distracted. Good thing. Otherwise, I'd sit around dreaming of how things might turn out between Khol and I. There was something oddly appealing about matchmaker spirits. They'd taken the dating app stuff out of the equation and paired us. It was up to us now to see if their prediction that we were fated mates was right or if throwing us together like this had been a huge mistake.

If nothing else, I could already see that Khol wasn't the type of guy to lure me in, then smirk and stride away.

I dressed in my bathing suit and stood for a moment, staring down at my body in the skimpy bikini the water spirit had provided. Some of my baby belly pooch remained. No matter how I dieted or how many crunches I did, I remained soft in that area. And frankly, sit-ups sucked. Who actually liked doing them?

I had stretch marks and not only on my belly. My hips had been happy to expand along with the rest of me, and the fine strips on the top of my ass had to be unattractive.

When I went to the pool with Flora to give her swimming lessons, I wore a one-piece. I hadn't cared how I looked. I was there with a bunch of moms who probably felt as awkward in their skin as me, and not one of us was going to point out someone else's flaws even if we saw them.

My thighs were too big, my boobs hung lower than I liked, and my—

Hold on right there. When had I started thinking my physical appearance mattered? I mean, it did to some extent, but my true worth wasn't in whether or not I had stretch marks on my belly but in the part of me I sheltered within my heart. Good looks didn't last forever. A body changed over time. There was no stopping age and with it came wrinkles and gray hair. Saggy things.

I needed to focus on what my body offered rather than what it didn't. I was strong. I could carry Flora for miles if I had to. And I had great balance. I might trip over something, but I didn't fall. My eyes didn't need correction—

thank the house spirit for that, because I wasn't sure where I'd find glasses or contact lenses here.

Khol found me attractive. I thought he did, that is. He seemed to.

So rather than ask the water spirit for a less revealing outfit, I thrust my shoulders back, secured my hair in a ponytail at my nape, and with a few cloths from the bathroom in my hand, I strode from the room.

I came to a halt when I saw Khol, who must've gone outside to change. Who would've thought a guy wearing only a scrap of fabric secured around his waist could be so hot? I'd seen him the day we arrived—drooled over him if I was being honest. Since then, he'd dressed in pants and tunics, hiding all his gorgeous blue skin and muscles.

He sat on the sofa with Flora nestled beside him, turning the pages of a book while she told him what the words said.

Did Zuldruxians read? I'd have to ask, though I hadn't seen any books around outside the ones the house had provided for Flora.

His muscles rippled with more muscles, from his neck all the way down to his calves. I ached to run my fingertips across his abs and massage his thighs. Stroke his pecs and trace my palms across his broad shoulders.

He'd left his silver hair down, and it hung thickly around his face, the tips brushing his shoulders. I loved his blue skin and the way his dark blue eyes contrasted so nicely.

He must've sensed me watching, because he lifted his head and flashed me a smile full of enough happiness to spill over to me.

And when his gaze traveled down my frame, his eyes smoldered.

Okay, he really did find me attractive.

With my head high, I walked over to stand beside the sofa. "Are you two about ready? It's steamy, and I can't wait to jump into the pool."

"Swimmin'," Flora cried, sliding off the couch. She held out her hand to Khol. "Come on, Khol. We gotta go right now."

"You're right. We've got to go right now." He chuckled and took her hand, and struggled to get up, implying that she actually was making a difference with her pull.

She sent me a smug look over her shoulder. "I's helping Khol."

"You sure are." Tipping my head back, I squinted up at the ceiling. "Hey, house spirit, could we have some sandals?"

A long pause followed where the god must be consulting whatever system it used to find us on Earth. Did they have an alien equivalent to computers? They must, because three pairs of flip-flops oozed up from the floor.

"Pink," Flora squealed, rushing over to sit beside her pair and tuck them onto her feet. She stood and gazed down at them. "Pwetty. So pwetty."

"I don't believe I've ever worn anything that looked like that before," Khol said, clearly skeptical. "But I'll try."

After studying Flora's feet, he slid his into one sandal after another, wincing when the thong tucked itself against his toes. He had cute toes with blunted nails like a human. No claws. His species mustn't need them on this planet.

Khol took the towels from me and laid them over his shoulder. Holding both our hands, he led us to the door that I opened.

Outside, a warm but stiff wind hit us.

Khol paused and peered at the sky. "The storm will be here soon."

"When?"

He shrugged. "Tonight, tomorrow? I'm not exactly sure."

Just in time for Christmas?

Unease slithered through me, and my skin peppered with goosebumps despite the tropical heat. "Do you get hurricanes here?" I explained what they were.

"Yes, though not often." He nudged his head to the right. "We go this way. Let's swim and enjoy the rest of our day. The storm will come when it must."

"It's windy now. Will it get worse?"

"Perhaps. Wind is common here on the island. It sweeps off the sea that stretches away from my island forever." His soft smile rose. "Not actually forever, though it seems so. Those of the Dastalon Clan who ride enormous birds called ryvars have traveled far beyond my island. They say there are large land masses in that direction. I asked if they encountered any people, but they said no. They didn't remain for long, however, so to this day, no one knows if anyone lives there."

"Would you ever like to travel there?"

He shot me a smile as we walked along a narrow trail leading through spindly woods with the stream on our left. A large pool of lavender water gleamed ahead, and the rush of the falls grew louder. "I can't imagine traveling that far with a raft, and I don't have a ryvar any longer. I had to leave him when I moved away from the Dastalon Clan."

"Was he a pet, someone you miss?"

"Very much so." He gazed toward the sky, and there was something so desolate and lonely about him that I wanted to hug him. Kiss him again. Tell him that he didn't always have to be alone.

Instead, I kept walking. We were dancing around each other, each testing the water before plunging in. That didn't mean we had to declare feelings or take this any further. For now, I'd see what happened next and not try to analyze it. Because Khol was special, I was beginning to believe I would rather stay here by his side than travel to settle in a different clan.

We stopped beside a pool that had to be thirty feet across. It looked deep, though shallow along the sandy shore. Trees of varying heights grew in clusters on the opposite side, draped with vines and peppered with thick clumps of shrubs covered with flowers. The shrubs marched down to the other shore until they reached the water. It had taken some time, but I was getting used to purple water and vegetation. I suspected it was no different than our shades of brown and green other than color.

"I should've asked the house spirit for a life jacket for Flora," I said, worrying my lower lip. "She's just learning to swim, and she's much too bold."

"Like her mother," Khol said with a smile. He tossed our towels over a shrub and scooped up my daughter. "I'll keep a hand on her at all times." With that, he strode into the water, Flora squealing with joy and me following.

I fretted but not for long, because I trusted him. He cradled Flora in his arms and carefully advanced into the water, first letting her touch her toes, which brought out her giggles, then slowly going deeper.

Because he was focusing on her, and I knew he'd give his own life to protect my child, I dove into the water and swam below the surface, coming up to watch them slowly join me.

While I couldn't touch where I was, Khol could. He stopped beside me, giving me a shy smile, and held Flora in the water.

She splashed her arms and kicked her feet. "Let go a me, Khol. Let go!"

"She does okay," I said.

"I'm going to hold onto the back of your swimming outfit, Flora," he said gently. "When you show me that you can swim, I'll let go."

Her little mouth twisted, and she huffed. "I's can swim. Really."

"Sort of," I said. "This is Khol's pool, so we follow his rules."

"Hate rules," she said with a sigh, but she gave in.

While I treaded water beside him, he slowly released her. She was soon paddling around us, huffing in the water with her eyes sparkling with excitement.

"Fun, Mommy. I love swimmin'."

"I do too, sweetie."

"You do so well," he said, keeping his hand near her in case she ran into trouble.

"I's do," she piped up. "I's swimmin'."

She doggie paddled around us while we savored the cool water. The wind kept gusting, making the tallest trees sway.

"What will we do if a hurricane's coming?" I asked. Oh, to have a weather station to consult right now.

"Make sure there's nothing loose outside for the wind to pick up and steal or slam into my house," he said. "I'll cover the windows to keep out the rain. And we'll stay inside when it hits."

So few options to escape what could be a furious storm.

"Should we go to shore? It might be safer on the mainland."

"We'll be safe here. I promise."

But his eyes drifted toward the sky, and his frown deepened.

CHAPTER 18

KHOL

We swam for a long time but as the sun started to set, we left the water. After drying off, I carried Flora while Nancy walked beside me.

"We're wet," she said before we entered the house. "Give me Flora, and I'll take her inside where we can both get out of our wet things and into something dry."

I held the cloths out to her, and she wrapped one of them around her daughter, bustling her inside to her bedroom. Their laughter rang out, and soon, Flora appeared from her room dressed in another pink gown.

She hurried over to stand in front of me. "I's hungry."

"Then let's feed you. More nuggets?"

"I's want fish."

Now that was a change. "Fish it is, then." I'd reset my water traps last night and this morning, before they got out of bed, I'd collected my catch. After cleaning them, I'd placed them in the cold box provided by the water spirit. "How should I cook it?"

She shrugged.

"I could fry it."

"That sounds wonderful," Nancy said, striding out of my bedroom. She wore only a simple, sleeveless lavender gown that dropped to just below her knees, and I'd never seen anyone prettier.

What would it be like to claim what the water spirit offered—what Nancy might be offering? She hadn't kissed me by accident. Where did she want this to go between us?

I'd loved Weela. There was no denying that.

But I could now see there was room in my heart for more than one person.

Nancy.

Flora.

If I stepped off the cliff and gave this a chance, I could have a family. I wouldn't be lonely any longer. I could cling to the hope for a wonderful future with them by my side.

If only I dared.

"What would you like me to cook with the fish?" she asked. "Tubers?" She lifted the ones I'd dug on the side of the stream. "They look vaguely like potatoes, which is promising."

"We could slice them and fry them with the fish. And ask the water spirit to give us other vegetables to round out the meal."

"What about donuts?" Her eyes sparkled with humor.

"They're awfully sweet." So was she. My heart kept dancing around in my chest, and if I let it free, I had a feeling it would fly through the roof and into the sky. Would it ever return to my chest again? I bet Nancy could snatch it from the sky and hold it tight and then it would belong only to her.

"What is it about our bodies craving sweet and salty stuff?" she asked.

"It tastes good."

"So does fish." She pointed to it sitting on the counter. "As do most desserts. Bread. Oh, yeah, bread," she breathed. "I miss bagels and cake and all sorts of floury treats."

"Vanessa makes bread. It's amazing. I couldn't stop eating it. And butter. They make that with hepadon milk."

"Really? Are they similar to cows?" She described the creatures.

"More or less. I believe our hepadons are bigger than your cows. At least twice as big. We ride them." I dredged the fish through a milky liquid I obtained by pressing a certain plant that grew in the jungle, then dipped it in something like the flour Nancy used to make clay. I'd added spices and my belly growled in excitement already. "Actually, *I* don't ride hepadons, but those in the Indigan Clan do. They use them for transportation."

"While you fly on ryvars."

"I used to. No more. After what happened, I can't return to the Dastalon Clan again, not if I wish to hold my head high."

"You should never be ashamed of loving someone."

"Our love hurt my friend. It hurt Weela."

"Your friend accepted your apology. He forgave you." Her gaze sought mine. "If Weela was alive, would she forgive you too?"

"Of course."

"How long has it been since she died?"

"Three years."

Nancy slowly nodded before her gaze sought mine again. "How long will you keep beating yourself up about it? It's been a long time."

"When she was murdered, I wasn't sure how I'd go on. Yet I've found the strength to do so."

"Pain does fade, though it never goes away."

For the first time since I left, when certainty blazed in my heart, I wondered about my actions. "Perhaps I should've remained there and accepted the judgment of my clan. Instead, I ran." I placed the long slices of fish in the heated oil. They sizzled, and their heady spicy scent filled the room.

"Sometimes, we have to separate ourselves from the situation to put it into the proper perspective. You both followed your heart, and others were hurt. She paid the ultimate price, but it seems like you did too."

"I did." I missed her, but over time, my feelings of guilt had faded. "Why didn't I want to follow her into death? Others often follow their mates."

"Only you can answer that question."

Why did the thought of losing Nancy gut me so much more than losing Weela? I'd loved her. Back then, it was all I could do to go on. Yet I had. I'd strode away from my clan and found a new life, one where I was content.

Weela and I were young back then. Were we too young to fall in deep love?

"My life has changed since I came to this island," I said. "I took my sadness and turned it into a new life."

"Are you happy?"

"I'm content." I was now happy because Nancy was here, and what did that tell me?

That I was falling in love, that maybe I did deserve a new mate. Could I accept that feeling in my heart?

"I'm looking forward to meeting the other women," Nancy said, placing the last of the tubers in the pan to boil.

"They'll be excited to see you."

How could I take her there and leave her? Even the thought of it made my hands shake.

Saying goodbye was going to rip through something vital inside me.

I turned the fish to cook it on the other side, focusing on this task and asking the house spirit for other vegetables and not the future I had no control over.

"What else does Vanessa make?" she asked as the water around the tubers came to a boil.

"Rolls with a sweet, spicy flavor. Seen-a-mon?"

"Cinnamon rolls? I'm dying to eat them already. Funny how deprivation sparks the appetite more than regular old hunger."

The women had traveled for a very long time, though none of us knew exactly how long. They'd remained in stee-sas . . . No stasis, per Vanessa. That was her assumption since they woke and no one on her planet knew about mine.

"Leave it to us to bring carbs with us." Nancy shook her head. "Did you enjoy her rolls?"

"Very much."

"Then I bet you'll enjoy the sugar cookies we'll make. I can't believe our Christmas is the day after tomorrow." She bit down on her lower lip. "It feels real, yet it doesn't. As I said, I lived in a place where it got very cold in the winter. We have lots of snow and that feels more seasonal to me, though I know many on my planet who also celebrate do so in the heat or whatever season it is in their part of the world."

"I believe we might have snow on Zuldrux. On clear days, I've seen mountains far in the distance, and they're capped with white."

"Maybe you'll travel there someday."

"I doubt it. I like it here on my island." Where I'd finally found peace.

"I have one big concern about Christmas," she said, still pensive. "Presents, though I plan to ask the water spirit to help with that. I don't know why it feels like cheating to ask the spirit to give them to me. It's no different than going to a store and buying them. Long ago, on Earth, people made their gifts by hand. It was a simpler yet more complex time."

"Here, we make whatever the gods don't give us. If you'd like, we could make some things for Flora together." I tugged the fish from the oil and placed the thick slices on our plates while she drained the tubers.

"I'd like that. Maybe after she's in bed tonight?"

"Of course. A grain dish, if you please," I said with a lifted voice, and a bowl of my favorite appeared on the counter to the right of our plates. "You're going to love this one. I eat it often."

She sniffed it. "It smells amazing. I think I'll love it too." She served each of us some of the grains, making up our plates with tubers and the other vegetables as well.

The fish was nearly done.

"I's hungry," Flora said, dancing over to stand beside us. Her pink gown had been adorned with real flowers. They'd wilt, but the water spirit would make another gown just like it. How long had it been since the water spirit could indulge a youngling?

"Get in your seat, then, sweetie," Nancy said.

Flora scampered over to the table, and I followed with two plates, placing the one with the smallest serving where she'd sit, then lifting her to settle her in her chair that shrunk to accommodate her tiny frame.

Nancy followed with the last plate, putting it on the table.

We sat and ate, laughing about this and that.

"I gotta make pwesents," Flora said after our empty plates had been absorbed into the table. "I don't have 'em."

"We can do that tomorrow," Nancy said, her gaze meeting mine. "I'm not sure what we can make, but we'll figure it out. This is going to be the best Christmas ever."

It was.

I was going to make sure of it.

CHAPTER 19
NANCY

We put Flora to bed, each of us telling her a story, then went out to the living area, shutting her door behind us.

The wind howled outside, telling me the storm had arrived, but we were safe and comfy inside Khol's snug home.

"Do you have a better idea now for how long the storm will last?" I asked as I collected Flora's toys and books and placed them in the wooden box.

"A day or more. I sense it's a big storm."

I dropped down onto the sofa, and he joined me, both of us staring forward. I wasn't much of a TV person, but right now, I'd welcome one if only to distract me from how amazing he smelled, how warm his body was sitting close to mine, and how my heart kept flipping around just because our thighs were touching.

I'd gone from worrying about falling for someone who'd treat me like Richard to falling for Khol who was nothing like the other man. My feelings were changing. He'd plunged into the sea to save us from a pack of sharknados. He'd done all he could to make my daughter happy. He was kind and considerate and thoughtful.

Our kiss had just cemented the feelings in my mind.

I wanted another kiss, but I wasn't sure how to ask. He'd loved someone deeply, and he was still working through her loss. He might never have room in his heart for someone new.

Without intending to, I'd slipped from liking into something precariously close to love.

Why had I let it happen? I gnashed my teeth and fisted my hands on my thighs. I was a fool. I'd told myself I'd never trust anyone again after what happened. That mistake had given me a precious gift in Flora, but it had also broken my heart.

Or had it?

When was the last time pain had stabbed through me when I thought about Richard?

Not since I was on Earth.

Sometime between focusing on the upcoming birth of my child to caring for her as a single parent, I'd fallen out of love with him. Coming here and meeting Khol had shoved Richard farther away, not only physically but emotionally.

Had I actually ever loved him, or had I been in love with the idea of being in love with someone?

The feelings churning through me right now were stronger than what I'd had for Richard. Sharper. And I suspected much more lasting. Leave it to me to truly fall in love with another male who might never fully want me.

"What's wrong?" he asked.

"Nothing." My shoulders curled forward. I couldn't speak. It was all I could do not to cry. Why did I do this to myself again? I thought I'd learned my lesson with—

He cupped my face and gently turned it, making me look his way. "Tell me."

"You love Weela."

"I did love Weela."

See? "You'll always love her. She was your fated mate. The only woman you'll ever adore."

"Nancy." When I continued to stare at his chest, he tipped my chin up. "Look at me. See me when I speak to you."

I didn't dare. Couldn't he just let me wallow in my misery?

"I loved Weela," he said. "You're correct."

"She was amazing."

"She was . . . a challenge."

"What?" Surprised, I looked up. He stared at me with so much warmth that it stole the breath from my lungs. "What does that mean? If you loved her, she was flawless, everything you could have ever dreamed of in a woman."

"No one is flawless; especially me. Yes, I thought she was perfect. Time can change perspective. I knew back then but ignored that Weela was self-centered. She wasn't mean. I don't say that. But she was young. I was too, a year younger than her."

"How old are you now?"

"Twenty-six."

"I'm thirty. Does that bother you?"

His head tilted, and he frowned. "Why would it?"

"Never mind." Jeez, I had it bad. He wasn't interested in me that way, so he wouldn't care that I was four years older than him. "Tell me more about Weela."

"Her parents indulged her and her older brother adored her. I loved her as well, as a fated mate always does—"

"Wait, what?"

"As a fated mate always does," he said gently.

"You're compelled to love your fated mate?"

"A fated mate is a gift." His sweet smile rose. "It's a joy to love the one you're fated to adore until your dying day."

"Weela."

He sighed. "I told you I loved her but . . ." His eyes closed and when he opened them again, I saw vulnerability there. A touch of sadness. And hope, something I'd lost when Richard walked out my front door. "I don't feel the same about her any longer. Is that bad?"

"I don't feel the same about Richard either."

"You loved him."

"Maybe? I thought I did then, but I know I don't any longer."

His eyes widened. "You're saying you have room in your heart . . ."

"For more than him? Totally."

"Nancy," he sighed.

What did that mean? "As for not feeling the same way any longer, no, it's not bad. I think life helps soften the rough edges. It has to, or we wouldn't be able to go on."

"I've finally put the feelings I had for her into perspective." His fingers traced down my arms, and I marveled that someone so big and muscular could be this tender. "Do you know how rare it is for someone to have two fated mates in their lifetime?"

"We don't have fated mates where I come from. Some people do love for a lifetime, though. We call them soulmates, but it's not the norm."

"The gods have been good to me. Weela might've been my first fated one, but she isn't my last. That's you, Nancy. You."

CHAPTER 20
KHOL

I was taking a big chance by sharing my feelings with Nancy, but I'd not only sensed her sadness, but it had also tugged me close to her. I wanted to hold her. Love her. And if one of us didn't take a chance and lay ourselves bare, we might never know where a life together might take us.

"Weela was special, but she's dead," I said. How could I explain it to her? "We were both young. Too young to be fated to spend a lifetime together. I wish her parents hadn't killed her, that they hadn't forced her to be with my friend, Nevarn."

"If they hadn't, you'd be with her now."

"Perhaps." I swallowed and the lump wouldn't go down. "I wish she was alive. But I can't imagine not meeting you. I don't compare you and her, not one bit. You're each special in your own way. But she's gone. I felt responsible for her death for a very long time, and that tainted my feelings for everything. You're right when you say I isolated myself to atone for my mistake. I felt it wasn't fair that I lived when she didn't."

"You left when they discovered who'd killed her."

"Do you know why?"

She shook her head, gazing up at me with what I prayed was affection in her eyes. "I assume guilt drove you."

We'd only known each other for a few days, but in some ways, it felt like a lifetime. When you knew, you knew.

Weela was my past, and Nancy was my future.

"Yes, I felt guilty. A need to be punished. But I now believe I needed this time to learn to forgive myself so I'd be ready for you." I laid my heart open to this precious woman who would either cup it gently in her tiny hands or tell me she'd never feel the same.

I'd survived Weela's death, but I knew right now that I would not be able to survive Nancy's rejection. What I felt for her was bigger than anything I'd experienced in the past. It encompassed all of me.

"I don't know what you're saying." Nancy's voice came out thready, as if I'd stunned her. "You loved her. You'll always love her." She tapped the mating mark on her hand. "This is a mistake. The gods will see they messed up and remove it."

"And what about mine?" I tapped the one on my arm that matched hers. "Was that a mistake as well?"

"Well . . ."

I held her face, making her look at me. "You're mine, Nancy."

The strips of hair above her eyes lifted. "I belong to no one but myself."

"You're mine. To love and to adore until our dying day."

"It doesn't work like that."

"Why not?"

"Water flowing beneath a house doesn't get to decide who I love or who you belong with."

"You're right."

Her breath whooshed out. "See? I'm right. It was a mistake."

Leaning close, I captured her mouth, kissing her hard, putting all of myself into it. When I lifted my head, she trembled and the heat in her eyes . . . If only I could claim it as my own. "We are not a mistake. I'll never believe that."

"You can't love me."

"I don't."

She sucked in a breath, and her eyes widened.

"But I will. I feel so much for you already. You're everything to me already, and we've only known each other for a few days. Don't throw away what we're building together. Give it a chance to grow and flourish. Please."

She jerked out a nod. "I don't know what's happening between us, but I like it. It's overwhelming, consuming, and scary."

"Loving someone can just about kill you, but it's also the purest, most wonderful feeling in the world. I want to share it with you, Nancy. You. Not anyone else and with no expectation but being together however the fates intend."

"I want you," she said. "You're right. We don't know where this will go, but I need to give it a try."

My smile made my face ache.

She rose up onto her knees, facing me and cupped my cheeks. "I'm going to kiss you, Khol. I don't know how far I want to take this tonight, but I'm not going to analyze it. Let's see where fate takes us, okay?"

I nodded. "You're special, Nancy. Never forget that."

Falling for this woman would be a gift I'd be foolish to throw away.

Her mouth claimed mine in a kiss that flamed through me. My cocks rose, pressing against my pants while her lips whispered across mine.

I kissed her back, putting my heart and my soul into it. I could shout to the world that I wasn't in love with her, but my soul already knew. This had nothing to do with us being fated. She was sweet perfection, my perfect fit, and I ached to show her.

Because she was so precious, I'd take care. Flora's father had hurt her, and I'd sacrifice myself before doing anything that might cause her pain.

Her lips parted, and she released a moan that shot right to my core.

My cocks smacked against my pants, wanting her. I ached to be with her fully.

It was crazy. I'd only met her a short time ago, but it felt like I'd known her forever.

I deepened our kiss, gliding my tongue into her mouth. She tasted sweet. Like berries, arousal, and life. Her hands gripped my shoulders tight, and she wrapped her legs around me, pumping her hips up against my abs.

Everything inside me ached to create something lasting and special with this woman alone.

Gone and with no desire to find myself again, I laid her back onto the couch.

Falling for someone meant taking a risk. I'd lost my family, my first mate, and my life in the clan I was born into. But if I didn't snatch what I could from what the fates offered me, this second chance, I'd miss out on something special.

For now, I'd let fate decide. If we were meant to be together, things would continue like they had with us getting to know each other, laughing and exchanging warm touches. If life had something else in store for us, at least I'd know I gave us a chance.

Continuing our kiss, I crawled up over her, bracing my palms on the couch on either side of her shoulders.

I left her mouth and kissed down her throat while she bucked up against me. She clung to me, her breathing ragged.

When I slid my fingers beneath her shirt and teased them across her belly and higher, she nudged me up only to pull off her top and toss it aside.

I feasted my eyes on her breasts. Zuldruxian females had no nipples, and I couldn't stop staring.

"They're pert," I said.

A smile quivered across her lips. "It doesn't take much friction to make my nipples ache. Touch them if you want. Suck on them. That feels amazing."

I nodded and dove down, tugging one nipple into my mouth while stroking my fingertips across the other. Touching her in this way sent heat roaring through me. I'd never felt this way about intimacy before. Never. And that told me how wonderful this moment between us was already.

She clung to my shoulders, pumping her hips up against my leg. Heat coiled tightly inside me; a wild thing that was determined to be set free.

I traced my fingers down her belly and cupped her between her legs. When she bucked up against me, I looked up and released her nipple. "Can I taste you?"

She nodded. "Yes. Yes!"

I didn't need more than that.

After gently removing her clothing, I crawled down between her legs and ran my fingertip through her wetness. She wanted me, and there was nothing more humbling for a male than that.

When I dipped my finger inside her, my groan ripped out.

Lifting my head, I watched her face as I slid my fingers in and out of her passage.

"Tell me what you like," I said.

"What you're doing is amazing. Touch my clit, though, if you want things to get really wet."

I loved how she could smile about this. And I loved it even more that she was eager to tell me how to please her.

"This?" I rolled her clit.

Her moan echoed around us. She lifted her legs, bracing her heels on the couch, and thrust up to meet my fingers. "More, more."

"And this?" I slid more fingers inside her and rubbed my thumb against her clit. "You take my fingers so well. Amazing," I purred.

She gasped and rocked against me, her breathing feverish and her hands fluttering by her throat. "I'm going to come, Khol. So fast and so hard."

"Take it, sweet. Let me feel your body give into my touch."

Her eyes slid closed as she gave into the feelings I created in her body.

"Tell me how this makes you feel, Nancy. I need to know." I pulled my fingers out and pushed them back inside, twisting them to give her inner walls equal attention.

"Yes, yes, more."

I couldn't stop grinning. She was so responsive, so wonderful. "More of what, sweet?" I brought my fingers to a halt.

Her groan roared up her throat. "Don't you stop now! I

love what you're doing. That finger twist thing? Do more of it and do it faster."

"Like this?" I drove my fingers inside and pulled them out just as fast while twisting them.

"Khol!"

Leaning close, I sucked in her heady scent, then licked her clit, flickering my tongue across it before dragging it down to join in with my fingers. She tasted wonderful, and I needed more.

My cocks were on fire, but they could wait. Now was for Nancy, for making her shatter from my touch.

She went wild, lifting her hips while yanking on my hair, and I loved it. I slid my tongue through her folds before sucking on her clit, over and over while her whimpers grew louder, and her body started to shake.

And when she came, I drove my tongue inside her.

CHAPTER 21

NANCY

Khol was amazing. He'd done something for me very few other men had. Sure, they tried a little foreplay, but wait for me to come before adding cock action?

Never.

I flopped back on the couch, still clutching the ends of his hair, though I released them. "Sorry. I hope I didn't pull out too much." My giggle slipped out. I'd never giggled with a guy before but man . . . *Alien*, that is. I felt giddy after what he'd just done. "Thank you."

He licked his lips and tugged a blanket off the back of the sofa, laying it over me. "You're wonderful. I want to do that again."

Sitting, I tugged on my shirt, leaving my lower half covered with the blanket for now. I couldn't look away from the enormous bulge in his pants. "Your turn."

His eyes widened. "Not yet."

I blinked. "Are you . . . shy about this?" Oh, damn, maybe he didn't want more with me. There could be unknown Zuldruxian sexual social norms, and I may have just crossed the line.

His head jerked in the negative. "I . . ."

"Has anyone touched you other than yourself?" Surely his first mate—

"No. I told you we weren't together that way. I wanted her. I loved her. But I couldn't do that to my friend."

"Was there anyone else before her?"

"A few."

Acid gouged through my belly, but I shut it down. "This is us. We're not looking backward, only forward."

"Forward," he said softly, his lips curling up in the sweetest smile.

I wanted to crawl all over him, to show him the same wonderful feeling he'd just given me. So I did. I climbed onto him, straddling his lap. I tugged on his tunic. "Off."

"My chest doesn't—"

I placed my fingertip over his lips. "This is new for us. Let me play?"

"Of course." With shaky hands, he ripped his shirt up and over his head, chucking it aside while I took in his glorious muscles.

He must work out, unless this was just the basic muscle tone of a Zuldruxian. What an interesting theory. I'd think about it later. Now was for touching.

I stroked his neck, watching his face, and smiled when I took in his four nipples. "You have nipples. I thought you said females don't."

"They have four breasts, but no nipples. At the base of their mounds," he ran a fingertip along his chest, slicing across the area between his upper and lower nipples, "they have soft, flexible tubes. The tubes extend when they wish to nurse their youngling."

"Are multiple births a thing?"

"It's common for a female to have at least two at one time. Three or four, even."

"Identical?"

He shook his head. "Not as far as I know. Long ago, each cluster of younglings would be a mix of female and male, but in recent years, they're only male and they come in smaller numbers, often only one at a time. But they don't share identical features, if that's what you mean."

"Then I bet the female decides, and her body releases the number of eggs it feels it can carry to term."

He shrugged.

Enough science talk. As I'd said, I wanted to play. I teased his nipples, gently rolling them before leaning close to lick them.

His breath caught. "That ..."

When I sucked one into my mouth, his head fell back against the sofa, and his groan ripped out. He stroked my head and back, and I adored how he was panting already.

While I continued to suck one nipple after the other, making all four bead, I traced my palms across his rippling abs. Truly, a woman could spend hours just touching them, gliding the tip of her finger along each groove. But I wanted to unwrap my next present.

I fumbled with the fastening to his pants until he gently nudged my hands aside and released it. The buttons below were easy enough to figure out, and I soon undid each one.

His cocks sprang free, a large one with a smaller one above it.

"Two," I exclaimed, gaping at the girth and length of the large one. It would fit inside me, but just barely. And oh, how amazing it was going to feel. Frankly, I couldn't wait, though I was going to make myself do so until at least tomorrow night.

Maybe.

"Two for your pleasure," he growled.

I loved how he was coming undone already, and I couldn't wait to make him fall apart in my arms—hands, that is.

"What's the smaller one for?" I asked as I wrapped my fingers around his big cock.

His guttural groan rang out. "It loves your clit."

"In what way?"

"Get rid of the blanket, and you'll find out."

I was as open to experimentation between the sheets as the next woman. A tug, and I tossed the blanket aside, revealing how wet I already was.

Then I got to work on his big cock. If the smaller one wanted to join in and do whatever it could offer, it was welcome. I was focused on giving my male pleasure.

When had I started thinking of him as mine?

Almost from the moment I met him.

As I milked his cock with my hands, he groaned, his head tipped back, and his eyes closed. "That feels amazing. Don't stop."

I grinned, loving that I could give him pleasure.

Leaning forward, he kissed me quickly, and I soon lost track of what I was doing. My hands slowed until I jerked back and shook my finger at him.

"No distractions. I'm busy."

"Yes, lovely one. Whatever you say," he bit out, his body tightening, and his cock surging up toward his abs.

I stroked his nipples with my tongue while pumping his cock. A bead of precum glistened on the tip, and I couldn't do anything less than lick it.

His muffled groan rang out, his hand pressed over his mouth to hold it back. I wanted to tell him to let it roar, that

I needed to hear him call out when he came, but the last thing we needed to do was wake up Flora. We'd be together one of these days but inside his bedroom and with the door shut. Thankfully, my daughter could sleep through almost anything.

Straightening, I continued licking his nipples while pulling hard on his cock.

His growls punctuated each stroke of my hand, and I'd forgotten all about his smaller cock until something probed between my legs.

I stared down, my eyes widening as the shorter cock stretched around the big one I was stroking and prodded between my legs.

"Wider," he bit out. "Spread your thighs wider, please, if you can."

What woman wouldn't respond to a request like that?

Anticipation was a wonderful thing. We were building something special between us, and I couldn't wait until we decided it was time to take this all the way.

The tip of his smaller cock grabbed onto my clit. My gasp rang out, and it was all I could do to focus when the tip started humming.

"It's . . ." I couldn't think. Couldn't speak. But I could move my hands, and I continued to stroke his cock, working from the base to the tip. Over and over while his smaller cock teased my clit.

"Is it oh-kay?" he asked, his hooded gaze meeting mine.

I could only jerk my head up and down in affirmation.

Soon, I was humping against him, my wetness smearing across his larger cock while the smaller one stretched to accommodate my movements.

I moved my hands faster, using the slipperiness I provided, and our muffled groans rang out.

And when he barked out a cry, his body jerking and his cock shooting into my hand, I let loose and gave way to my own orgasm.

I collapsed in his arms, then tipped my head back to look up at him.

"You're amazing," he growled, stroking my back. "Truly amazing."

CHAPTER 22

KHOL

I slept on the couch again. I wouldn't go to her bed until she invited me. And if she never did, well, I'd slept in worse places after leaving the Dastalon Clan and wandering across the sea on my raft.

When Nancy crept from my room early the next morning, I sat up and gave her a grin. If only I could lay her on the cushions and lick her again. But I wouldn't dare do anything like that when her youngling daughter might walk from her room and see us.

"Morning," Nancy said, and the light in her eyes when she looked at me stunned me. I didn't think she'd wake with regrets—not really. But I'd worried. Were we taking this too fast?

It felt right to me, but I respected that it might not be right to her.

She glanced at Flora's closed door before sauntering over to where I sat on the couch. Bracing my shoulders, she leaned into me and kissed me. "A very good morning."

"That it is." My face hurt from my smile's stretch. I held her hips, wishing I could draw her down onto my lap and show her pleasure once more. She deserved it every day of her life.

When Flora's bedroom door opened, Nancy eased away.

"Morning, sweetie," she said brightly. "It's Christmas eve. Well, tonight is Christmas Eve."

"Santa comes tonight." Flora danced over to stand by the sofa. "Will Santa come for Khol?"

"He sure will," Nancy said. "What would you like for breakfast? How do eggs sound?"

"Yum." After patting my arm, Flora rushed over to the table and climbed into her chair. "Can I have scwambled eggs?"

A plate eased up from the counter.

Nancy shook her head but smiled as she collected it and placed it in front of Flora. An eating implement appeared, and the youngling started eating, swinging her feet to the tune she hummed. After each bite, she sang a bit about a creature named Frost-ee, a male made of snow.

"What would you like, Khol?" Nancy asked, returning to the counter. "I think I want scrambled eggs too. Toast? Jam if you have it. And a big mug of hot tea."

"I'll have the same." I came up behind her and leaned over to kiss the side of her neck. That was all it took for my cocks to catch fire. I beat them down mentally, telling them to behave.

Leaving her plate where it was, Nancy turned in my embrace. "If you're a good boy, Santa will bring you a present tonight." Her sparkling eyes met mine.

"I'm always a good youngling," I said with a grin, kissing the tip of her nose. I wanted to shift her plate to the side, lift her up onto the counter, and step between her parted thighs, but I couldn't do that in front of Flora. Zuldruxian couples showed affection to each other often and when around others, but we didn't do anything inti-mate where others could see.

"If you bad," Flora chimed in around a bite, "you get coal. Ha. Coal for Khol! It funny, Mommy."

"It sure is." Nancy shot me a grin that made my heart roar and lowered her voice. "Show me how good you can be later?" She closed one eye, opening it quickly, and her grin told me this was part of her tease.

"I'm going to hold you to that, sweet," I said, kissing her mouth, wishing I could linger.

I stepped away from her and collected our plates, bringing them over to the table. We sat and ate as a family, and I couldn't be happier.

"After breakfast, we're going to make cookies," Nancy said. "Does your oven work when it rains?"

Even now, it drummed on my sturdy roof, but the wind had died down, and I was sure the storm would be nearly over before our special eve.

"I built it beneath an overhang on the back of my house," I said. "It'll work fine. We'll bake the coo-kees?"

She nodded, chewing her bite and swallowing. "After we finish them, I need some time alone."

"Why, Mommy?"

I cocked my head, curious as well.

"Christmas is coming. That's all I'm going to say." She looked my way and closed one eye again before opening it.

"Is your eye oh-kay?" I asked, concern growing inside me. Was she sick? I hadn't . . . hurt her last night, had I?

"My eye . . ." Her frown cleared, and her low laugh rang out, tickling down my spine. "I was winking. That means we're sharing a secret."

A secret?

"Ah," I said. I propped the lids of my right eye open and closed my left. "A secret."

Her laugh only grew louder.

"I need time too," Flora said. "I need ta make pwesents."

"We'll see what we can do, sweetie," Nancy said.

We finished our meals and went to the counter.

"Hey, smart house," Nancy said. "I don't suppose you could play some Christmas carols, could you?"

"Carol is a name, isn't it?" I asked, studying the mix of ingredients in the bowl that were supposed to be soo-gar cook-ees. I'd dipped my finger in the soo-gar, and its sweetness held promise. I was curious to see how we were going to turn this big mass of dough into individual bites, which was how Nancy described cook-ees.

"Yes, Carol is a name but, in this instance, it means music." Nancy sighed. "I don't think the water spirit knows any carols."

"We can sing, Mommy." Flora stood on her chair I'd pulled over to the counter, mixing the ingredients at her mother's direction. "Jingle bells, jingle bells," she cried out. "Jingle all da way!"

Nancy joined in, and after a few rounds of the lyrics, so did I, all of us laughing as we sang the carol.

I'd never had more fun in my life. Imagine, this could be my life every single day. Kissing Nancy in the morning, playing with Flora and being the male she needed as a father, and taking Nancy to bed each evening. Nothing could be better than that.

While our cook-ees baked and the storm continued to rage outside, we sat, snug inside the home I'd built myself, sharing stories. Nancy told us about a greench who hated Christmas and how he discovered he had a heart bigger than he'd ever imagined. I made up a story about a grundar who discovered Christmas for the very first time. I dreamed up the tale after Nancy shared that on Christmas eve, the animals could supposedly speak.

"Do grundars get out in da rain?" Flora stared out the front window at the rain coming down in torrents and the jungle trees swaying around us in a lavender wave. "They get wet."

"They'll be fine," Nancy said. "They have fur coats to keep them comfortable and warm."

Flora turned and stared at us with concern. "I want a grundar."

"You created a monster," Nancy said with a wink. I now understood the gesture, and while I couldn't do it myself, I was going to practice because I found it very appealing.

"I's not a monster." Flora stomped across the room and slumped on one of the smaller chairs in the living area. "I's a pwincess."

"It's a saying that means things are getting a little out of control."

"I's in control," she said, crossing her arms on her chest.

"Sometimes, I completely agree," Nancy said with a sigh. She stood. "We should check the cookies."

"I'll go with you." I'd do it myself and she could stay dry, but I wasn't sure how to tell if they were finished cooking.

We went outside and found the first batch of cookies ready to be removed from the oven. They smelled amazing, and I couldn't wait to taste them.

Flora stood inside the open doorway when we hurried in that direction, me holding the stone slab with the cook-ees while Nancy shielded them from rain with a big leaf. Wind gusts smacked my sides and back, and it was hard to keep the cook-ees from getting soaked.

Inside, Flora shut the door while we hurried to the kitchen. I laid the slab on the counter, and Nancy scooped the cook-ees off, placing them on a plate she requested from the water spirit. After, she loaded the slab with the final batch of cook-ees and we repeated the process, her covering them with a big leaf while I carried them out and placed them inside the oven.

We ate cook-ees, and they were the best thing I'd ever tasted.

"I could eat them all," I exclaimed.

"Save some for Santa," Flora said. "We need ta leave some for him tonight."

"Alright," I said with a dramatic sigh that made them laugh.

We spent the rest of the afternoon playing games, reading books, and telling stories.

"Normally, I'd be preparing my feast for tomorrow," Nancy said. "It's strange that I can ask someone else to present what I'd like to eat."

"What do you normally eat to celebrate the holiday?" I asked.

Flora slumbered, leaning against my side, her thumb in her mouth. We'd have to wake her for dinner soon, though I wasn't sure she'd eat much after the cook-ees.

"Ham or a turkey." Nancy stroked her daughter's hair. "Funny how your water spirit won't present us with meat yet the meals I always prepared for holidays centered around it. There are always side dishes, of course, but the presentation seems to be all about the dish of meat."

"I can hunt for something. Grundar, maybe. It's quite tasty when roasted."

"A grundar sounds a bit like an extra-large guinea pig to me. Kind of a pet." She grimaced. "I know I eat meat that comes from animals many consider pets. I guess I should think more about that."

"We need meat to remain strong."

"You're right. It's a source of protein, which is one of the nutrients in meat, but I feel better eating fish for whatever reason."

"I could set some traps near the shore and catch fish for tomorrow's meal. Or fish in the morning if the storm has ended."

She glanced toward the window where rain continued to pelt that side of the house exposed to the small meadow. "How much longer do you think the storm will continue?"

"I assume it'll end during the night, but sometimes, these things are hard to say."

"On Earth, we have technology that looks at satellite images and can give predictions about storms. We know they're coming days before they arrive." She explained how this was done, though she admitted she didn't have much science background, and she was sure her explanation wasn't quite correct.

"I can tell when a storm is coming by watching the sky and the creatures and vegetation around me. The beasts prepare as well, storing food in their burrows or building their nests higher. The vegetation responds to the wind. Someone once told me that when the leaves were turned upside down, it meant it was going to rain, and that's often true. I can also smell it coming in the air."

"That's amazing. You've heightened the senses that we, on Earth, tend to ignore."

"I'm grateful if it helps me keep you both safe." I looked down at Nancy, and my heart turned over. I adored her already in an almost overwhelming way. I would protect her until my dying day, shelter her in my arms and in my heart, and support her in whatever she chose to do. If she still wanted to go to the Indigan Clan to settle, I'd travel with her. She was my home and my heart, and I couldn't imagine trying to find happiness without her.

She gazed up at me, and I swore I saw the same feeling in her eyes. It heartened me, giving me hope that what we were building would only grow stronger.

"We should wake Flora," she finally said, sliding off the couch. "I'll make something to eat, though you should expect her to be sleepy and cranky. Or wound up like a spring. She's power-napping and the end result could be just about anything."

She stooped down in front of her daughter and stroked her face. "Sweetie? Time to wake up. We need to have dinner, and then you can go to bed."

"Don't wanna go to bed," Flora said, stretching. Her eyes opened, and she stared around. "Almost time for Santa. I's gonna wait for him."

Nancy's sparkling eyes met mine. "If he sees you're awake, he won't come."

"That's right," I said, rubbing the youngling's back. "Once he knows you're asleep, he'll slip into the living area and leave presents."

Ours already sat beneath our tree, and I'd never seen anything prettier—outside of Nancy and Flora—than the tree we'd decorated with ornaments made with love in our hearts.

"Okay," Flora said with a sigh. She slid off the chair and walked into the kitchen, climbing into her seat that shrunk to accommodate her tiny size. "I's want pizza!"

A dish slipped up from the counter, and I retrieved it, frowning at the circular food with a light base topped with splotches of various colors. "Here you go." I placed it in front of her.

"I's want peppa-oni," she wailed.

"It's a spiced meat," Nancy said. She rubbed Flora's back. "This cheese and veggie pizza looks almost as good. Try it; you might love it this way too."

"But der's no peppa-oni." She sniffed and swiped the tears off her face. After shoving the dish away, she dropped her upper body onto the table, sobbing about peppa-oni.

"Oh, dear," Nancy said with a wry smile. "Maybe order something else? The water spirit can cook you almost anything. That's a true gift."

Flora lifted her head, tears trailing down her pink cheeks. "Ice cweem. Cake. I want sompin' sweet."

"You can have another cookie for dessert, but no dessert until you eat at least a little dinner," Nancy said firmly. She lifted her voice. "I'd like a similar pizza, if you please." The dish appeared on the counter, and she brought it over, sitting across from Flora. Leaning forward, she sniffed the meal. "It smells delicious."

Flora heaved a sigh. "I's guess so."

"I'll have the same," I said, bringing my meal to the table and joining them. "It looks tasty." I lifted the entire thing, folded it in half, and took a big bite.

Flora gazed at me with wide eyes, her tears forgotten. "You gotta cut it."

"Why?" I asked, munching through the bite. It tasted wonderful. Vanessa had made pizza when I stayed with the Indigan Clan for a few days during my travels.

Even when I felt I didn't deserve anything further in life, I'd missed people. It was nice talking with someone other than myself, and I'd enjoyed soaking in their cave pools.

"'Cuz you do," Flora said. She frowned at her pizza. "Mommy, you gotta cut it."

Nancy collected one of my stone blades from the kitchen. I'd brought them with me when I left the Dastalon Clan who was supported by stone spirits. After slicing Flora's pizza, she took her seat again and did the same with her own meal.

Flora lifted a triangular chunk and bit into it. "It's okay," she huffed. "Needs peppa-oni."

"It's yummy," Nancy said around a bite. "This vegetable," she pointed to a circular slice, "has a spicy flavor a lot like pepperoni. And no pig had to die to make it."

"Pigs die for peppa-oni?" Flora gaped down at her pizza before pushing it away again. "I can't eat cute pigs!"

She burst into tears once more.

CHAPTER 23
NANCY

"Someone's very tired," I said.

"I's not tired," Flora dramatically wailed. "I just slept. And I's can't eat cute piggies."

"No pigs died to make this pizza. It's all vegetables and grain. Cheese on the top. I think. It tastes like cheese, that is." I nudged my chin toward her meal. "Finish up, and you can take a nice bath."

"Can we go swimmin'?" she asked Khol.

"Not during the storm." His gaze cut to the window.

It still rained outside, though the wind gusts weren't hitting the building with as much force. Maybe it would end tonight, like he said. Who needed a meteorologist when we had Khol?

"Tomorrow," he told her. "You can swim after we go fishing for our dinner."

"Fish for Christmas?" she asked. "I want turkey. Ham. No, no. I don't want those. They're friends." Her sobs had stopped but she still appeared as dejected as if her entire life had been ripped out from beneath her, which I suppose it had.

"I'll make it taste amazing," I said. "You're going to love it."

"Okay," she said with a sigh. "I miss my home. Dis isn't my home."

Khol's face fell.

She'd hurt him, but I didn't scold her. She was a child, and she had the right to miss the life she'd left behind on Earth. This was a major adjustment for me, and I was an adult. A child wouldn't see it the same way.

But I took his hand and squeezed it. "I love it here. Zuldrux is special, and so are you."

His smile lifted, though shadows still lingered in his eyes.

The water spirit removed our empty plates, and I took Flora to the bathroom, where I filled the tub. While she bobbed around and played in what looked like a six-person hot tub when compared to her, I told her more holiday stories. Cartoon shows had been a big thing for us back on Earth, and it would be wrong to say I wouldn't miss them. I'd tell her our favorites every year, though, and I bet this would start a new Zuldrux tradition. We'd incorporate Zuldrux culture into our own, and before long, it would feel seamless.

Funny how when I thought about creating a permanent relationship with Khol, I hadn't thought about how this would play out for my daughter.

Would she soon want to call him daddy? She'd asked about her father often, and I was as honest as I could be without painting myself a victim and her dad a horrible person. He hadn't wanted anything to do with her, but that wasn't a rejection of her, just the role of a parent.

After she was dressed in PJs, we left the bathroom, aiming for her bedroom.

"Need Khol kisses," she said, rushing over to stand in front of him where he sat on the sofa. "Kisses, Khol. Kisses!"

He scooped her up and cradled her in his arms, nuzzling her neck while growling. She squealed with laughter and kicked her feet.

He'd make a great dad. A wonderful husband and mate. A perfect companion to spend the rest of my days with.

Was I in love with him? Hard to say when we'd only been together a short time. But I liked everything that made up this special guy, and I could easily see myself beside him for the rest of my days.

Even better, he seemed to feel the same way.

The warmth I felt for him couldn't be denied. It was like a wave roaring toward the shore, determined to rush over me. I had a feeling I'd greet it with my arms open and my heart on fire.

When he lifted his head, he sent me a tusky grin that sunk right through me, warming me from the inside out.

Flora slipped from his arms and skipped over to me. "We gotta hang our stockings."

"You're right, sweetie." As I stroked her hair, I felt like crying, and I knew why. I was falling for him, but I wasn't sure I dared. Richard hurt me. Realistically, I knew they were two different men, but it wasn't easy to convince my heart that I could trust anyone.

Fortunately, I didn't have to decide right now. It was Christmas eve, and my little girl was excited. Tomorrow would be a slightly different day than the one we were used to, but it would be just as wonderful.

Maybe even better than wonderful, because we'd share it with Khol.

He got up off the couch. "I asked the house spirit to give us stockings, but I'm not sure it got it right." He tugged something out from behind him. Had he been sitting on them, hiding them for a surprise? The twinkle in his eyes said yes. "What do you think of these?"

The house spirit had created stockings very much like the ones we'd used at home, big red and green things that no one would wear but were perfect for filling with small treats. Each had our names in scrolling letters.

"Dis mine," Flora said, pointing. "Flora."

Back on Earth, we were working on her letters, something I'd have to restart here. Books would pose a dilemma. I was a big reader, but it wasn't like I could go to the bookstore or order some new reads online. No ereaders in sight.

Life on Zuldrux would be very different than the one we would've had on Earth. Better, though, I bet.

Since the house didn't have a fireplace—the water spirit kept the temperature even all year long—we hung our stockings on the back of the door. I was banking on the spirits helping me fill her stocking tonight, along with Khol's. As for his present, I had something in mind I hoped he'd been wishing for.

Me.

My veins felt all swirly and heady, as if I'd drunk a big glass of wine.

Tonight, I was going to suggest we take this farther.

From the moment I discovered I was pregnant and that I was going to be a single mom, I dedicated myself to being both parents for my daughter. As if I had to make up for Richard's lack. I'd scrimped on everything to make sure she had what she needed, both financially and otherwise. I assumed I'd continue to do so until she'd finished college and started her own life. Only then might I consider doing something for myself.

Even now, I'd make sure everything was perfect for Flora's Christmas before considering my own needs.

But tonight, after she'd gone to bed, I'd do something solely for me. My skin tingled at the thought.

Would Khol turn me down or grin and say, "It's about time"?

"We hafta put out cookies and milk for Santa," Flora said. "We gots cookies, but no milk."

"I bet Santa would love a nice hot mug of tea," I said. "And for his reindeer? I know they eat more than carrots. We'll ask the water spirit to give us a plate full of vegetables that suit reindeer."

"Yes," she squealed, rushing toward the kitchen.

Khol lifted his unibrow. "Carrots?"

"You'll see," I said with a smile. Now that I'd committed myself, my veins were on fire. I couldn't wait to melt into his arms.

The water spirit came through with a plate of mixed vegetables, a mug of tea, and an empty plate for a few of the cookies we'd made earlier.

With great ceremony, we put them on the table.

"Now I's gotta go to sleep or Santa will know I'm awake." Flora danced toward her room. "I can't wait for Santa to come for Cwis-maas."

Khol came along with us, a whimsical smile on his face. We both tucked her in and gave her kisses, and for tonight, she didn't want any stories.

"I's gotta go to sleep." She laid her clasped hands on her chest and closed her eyes. Her lips quivered with joy, and just seeing her happy made my heart soar. When I first got here, I was so worried about how we'd survive.

Now we had a new home with someone who cared for us.

I couldn't wait to start my new life with Khol.

We shut the door and walked over to stand near the sofa.

"Presents," I whispered. "Though we'll have to wait in case she gets up."

"Will she?" He kept his voice just as low. "I have a feeling she won't dare get up in case Santa sees."

"You're probably right."

He walked over to stand close to me, his fingers tentatively stroking across my face, smoothing hair behind my shoulder. "Shall we tell each other stories since we missed out?"

The smile teasing across his lips made everything inside me shimmer with joy.

"I was thinking . . ." I pinched my eyes shut before opening them again. It would be so easy to hide, to step away from him and continue denying myself something I wanted.

But no more. I'd done everything for my daughter. It was time to do something solely for me.

Well, me and Khol.

"I was thinking . . ." I said, my voice much too croaky.

His face going serious, he nodded, urging me to finish.

"I want to be with you, Khol. Completely."

CHAPTER 24

KHOL

"Could you clarify that?" I asked, my voice so raspy, I could use it to sand something smooth.

She stepped closer and gazed up at me. I saw so much hope and wonder in her eyes. Did any of that apply to me or was she just happy about the holiday we were giving her daughter?

"I want to be with you completely, Khol. That means you and me, in your bed with no clothing on."

"No clothing," I croaked.

"Well . . ." A frown took over her face. "Unless you don't want me that way."

"I want you any way you want to give yourself to me," I said, finally finding my voice. "I'm falling in love with you, Nancy, and all I can think about is touching you, doing things for you, holding you. I want to be your life and your future and everything in between. So, yes, I want to take you to my bed."

Her smile smoothed away her frown. "Then what are we waiting for?"

"Mate," I said. "Precious mate." I swept her up in my

arms and strode into my bedroom, shutting the door behind us. When I laid her on my bed, all I could see was her. She belonged here, in my arms and in my life forever.

And I was going to show her.

I climbed over her, caging her with my body, though one twitch, and I'd back away.

When she just stroked my arms and looked up at me, a smile teasing across her mouth, I couldn't resist kissing her.

Looking at her made everything inside me quiver. I wanted this moment, our first time, to be special. This woman meant everything to me. I couldn't imagine being without her. If only this time could last forever.

I claimed her mouth with my own, drinking from the passion she so readily offered.

Flames burst inside me, making my heart pound. I slid my tongue across the seam of her lips, and when she opened them for me, a groan ripped through me. She wanted me as much as I did her, and that humbled me. There would never be anyone for me but Nancy, but I was beginning to believe that I was all Nancy would ever need as well.

I slid my fingers into her hair, holding her head, angling it to deepen our kiss. With teasing strokes of my tongue, I drew out her passion, feeding both our needs at the same time.

Leaving her hair, I gently glided my fingers across her cheek and jaw. Down her throat to the sweet junction of her neck and her chest. My lips followed. I kissed from her ear to her chin while she clung to my shoulders.

"Khol," she breathed. "My Khol."

"My Nancy. My mate," I growled against her neck.

She nudged me up, and sat, tugging her tunic off and

tossing it aside. With a sultry smile, she laid back on the bed.

I'd craved her breasts from the moment I saw them, and this time was no different than the last. I ran my tongue across one ripe bud, then the other, bringing them both to hard peaks.

She arched her spine and tipped her head back, her eyes sliding closed as she gave in to her pleasure.

Needing her touch as desperately as I needed to touch and taste her, I tugged off my tunic, flinging it toward the wall. Just a few seconds away from her breasts was too much. I latched onto her nipple, nibbling gently while rolling the other between my fingers.

Heat spiraled inside me, and my cocks rose to press against my abs.

When she urged me up again, we both stripped everything else off quickly, smiling at each other while we did it.

"Show me," she whispered, sinking back into our bed, tugging me down on top of her.

Not without making sure she was ready. My fingers had been inside her, and while even thinking about that made me nearly come undone, I remembered how much smaller she was than me. The last thing I wanted to do was hurt her. I wouldn't drive my cock inside her until her body was as prepared as it could be.

I kissed across her belly and spread her legs, shooting her a grin. I still couldn't believe she wanted to be with me, that she cared for me. This was the start of us, and I wasn't going to waste one second.

Once I started licking, I couldn't stop. She tasted amazing. I would never get enough. While rubbing one nipple, then the other, I focused my tongue on her clit, licking before sucking it into my mouth, only to run my tongue across it again.

I slid a finger inside her, and when she clenched on it, I almost came right then. How was I going to hold myself back if her body did that to my cock?

My head burst up. "You need to be on the top."

"What?" She gave me a dreamy, happy look that gutted me. I was making her feel this way. Why was I stopping?

Oh, yes, right. "If you're not on top, I'm going to split you in two."

Her eyes widened, and I hated seeing her coming back into herself when I'd been so determined to give her that floaty feeling. "I doubt you're going to split me in two."

"It's a blade. It'll rip you asunder."

"It's a cock, not a chainsaw."

I had no idea what a chainsaw was but— "Maybe we shouldn't do it at all. I can stroke myself. You can do the same. We'll both find pleasure."

She sat up, her face scrunching. "I'd love to watch you jerk off, and I'll happily get myself off with you watching, but I think we're talking about two different things here."

"My cock is going to shred your insides." I felt frantic now, determined to protect this woman I adored above all others.

"Stop. You'll give me a complex." Her laughter burst out.

I joined in, though I wasn't sure what was so funny.

She cupped my face. "You're not going to hurt me. We'll take it slow and," her smile grew, "if you want, I'll be on top."

CHAPTER 25
NANCY

I loved how sweet he was, how caring, and how he was willing to sacrifice his own needs to keep me safe. I'd never met anyone like Khol, and I doubted I would again.

He was so easy to love.

I climbed off the bed and pointed to the headboard. "Sit up with your legs stretched out."

He did as I asked, his cocks jutting up from his groin, his face so open and sincere.

"You're not going to hurt me. We'll make sure of that," I said. "Do you trust me?"

He nodded earnestly, his brow tight with a frown and his lips compressed.

"I know what feels good and what hurts." With that, I climbed onto his lap, straddling him. I rose up onto my knees and curled my finger for him to lower his head. "I need kisses."

His lips twitched. "You can have whatever you need, mate."

"You, Khol. I need you."

That frown reappeared on his brow. "We don't dare try."

"If we don't try, we'll never know if it will or won't work. But I won't force this. If you don't want to then—"

He tilted my chin and kissed me, breaking through my train of thought. All I could focus on was him. His mouth was pillowy soft, and his tusks only firm on my chin. And when his tongue slid into my mouth, I met it with my own. I clung to his shoulders, rocking my body against his. Each thrust rubbed my clit against his larger shaft, and I couldn't wait to feel it sinking inside me.

We burst apart and just stared at each other, lost in this moment and what might come next.

"I do want you. More than anything." His fingertips delicately teased from my shoulders to my breasts. "These are lovely," he rasped, his gaze locked on mine. He lightly pinched my nipples, sending shockwaves to my clit. I throbbed for him there, and with each push against him, I coated his length with my wetness. "You're perfect." He leaned forward to suck one nipple into his mouth.

The heat roaring through me made me want him with an insatiable need.

And when his second cock wove around the large one and latched onto my clit, it was all I could do to hold myself back.

"Now, Khol," I said. "I need everything."

Shadows filled his eyes, but he nodded.

Lifting up, I took the head of his cock and placed it at my entrance, shifting it back and forth to coat it with my wetness. I was panting already, trying not to give way to the pleasure roaring through me.

"Watch," I whispered.

His gaze slid down my frame in a caress, and he placed

his hands on my hips. Would he hold me back or give into his need to thrust me down onto his length?

I pushed down, taking the head of his cock inside me, and what an amazing feeling. Yes, he was thick and long, but we were going to make this work.

"Are you with me?" I asked, struggling not to moan at the exquisitely lovely feeling.

At his nod, I lifted my body up and let my weight shove me down, taking more of him inside me, pressing my face into his chest.

His groan echoed around me, and his second cock started humming faster.

"Slow that baby down," I said, my voice muffled against his chest.

"You tell me when," he said as his smaller cock stopped vibrating. It clung to my clit and that was enough for now. I walked on the edge and too much stimulation would send me tumbling down the side. I wanted him with me when that happened. And I wanted to feel all his cock inside me —or as much of it as I could take.

"You're mine," I growled.

His lips twitched upward. "I am."

"I'm going to claim you." Rising, I dropped down hard, wiggling to take more of his length.

Despite the trembling of his body as he held himself back, his smile grew. "You are."

"Don't deny me."

"Never."

"When I push down next, I need you to help."

He studied my face. "I'm not ripping you apart?"

"Not so far. I'll let you know." I was so close. But I needed to feel all of him before I gave way.

I rose and dropped, this time with him pushing on my hips.

"Thrust up next time." So close. So close! I was a shaking wreck, my clit on fire and the rest of me craving that rush only this male could give.

"Alright." He said it seriously, as if I'd asked him to do something he equally feared and anticipated. His body shook too. We were a mess, but we were messing things up together.

"Next time, you're going to thrust a few times, slowly, and then hard, got it?"

He grinned, flashing his tusk. "Got it."

"On three, push up when I drop down."

"On three."

I counted down to one and oh, my . . .

I paused with him fully seated inside me. His hands trembled on my hips, and his cock throbbed, twitching just enough to drive me closer to the edge.

"I'm going to be finished fast," I said. "Are you with me?"

"If you move much more, it's all over for me."

We both burst into laughter.

And then I started moving, lifting and falling while he drove up to meet me. We went faster, clinging to each other, our gazes locked as we rode each wave toward the shore.

Our bodies slapped together, and I couldn't imagine anything better than being with this man here and now. My moans echoed his groans, and our bodies shook.

And when his second cock started humming again, I tumbled hard down the other side.

His shout of joy rang out as he followed me onto the shore.

CHAPTER 26
KHOL

I hadn't ripped her apart. She'd found pleasure. And me? I'd fallen completely in love with this woman. It wasn't just the amazing sex; it was her. The softness of her touch. The way she looked at me as if I was all she'd ever need. The way she so willingly shared her daughter with me.

We slept in each other's arms, but only for a short time.

"Presents," she finally said. "Then you're going to ride me. Will you do that for me, Khol?"

"I'll try." My laugh burst out along with hers. We'd more than tried and it had been amazing.

We slipped from the bed, and I helped her dress in a soft gown that only came to her mid-thighs. She wore nothing beneath and that was all I was going to be able to think about.

What we'd done . . . I held her face as she gazed up at me so sweetly, and I thanked the fates and anyone who might be listening for bringing this woman to me. For the first time since I couldn't remember when, I felt complete.

I kissed her, and it was hard to end it and step back. But I wanted to work with the house spirit to craft my own gifts. They needed to be under the tree when we rose in the morning.

Holding hands, we left the bedroom and went to the kitchen area, the best place to make requests of the house spirit.

"No peeking or listening," Nancy said with a smile. "Some of these things are for you." She cleared her throat. "House spirit? I'd like . . ." Leaning close to the counter, she whispered.

I did my best not to overhear and moved farther along the counter to do the same thing.

Each item emerged from the counter already wrapped in bright cloth. Smaller items were stuffed into the stockings.

After a short time, presents lay mounded beneath our pretty tree. We stood beside it, holding hands again, and sent each other grins.

Christmas was coming.

"To bed," Nancy announced, squeezing my hand. "You've got a promise to keep."

"One I can't wait to fulfill." Not long ago, I worried I'd hurt her. I should've trusted the clan spirit to send someone who perfectly fit into my life.

Two, with Flora. The child of my heart. The youngling of my soul. I would be the best parent possible.

We paused outside our bedroom.

"I'll peek in on Flora," Nancy whispered. "Wait up for me?"

"Always." I kissed her deeply, savoring the thrill rushing through me, the way my body had already started responding.

She stepped back and after giving my bare chest a caress, she opened Flora's door.

Her gasp rang out, and I joined her in the opening.

Flora wasn't in her bed.

CHAPTER 27
NANCY

"Flora," I cried out. "Flora!" I patted the bed, though she clearly wasn't lying on it. "Warm." She hadn't been gone for long.

Rounding the bed, I dropped to my knees and looked underneath. Not there.

My frantic gaze met Khol's. "Where is she?"

We searched the house, and when we didn't find her anywhere, we grabbed footwear and raced outside. The wind still howled, and it was darker than the inside of a pocket. No moon to light our way—or Flora's way.

"Flora," I shouted. "Flora!"

I couldn't hear anything over the rush of the wind and the sway of the trees around us.

"The pool." Had she gone swimming? It wasn't like her to get up on her own and leave the house. She'd never done anything like this before.

We ran to the falls but didn't find her there. The dread coursing through my veins only grew.

Gazing frantically around, we kept yelling her name.

She didn't come to us.

"My baby. Where's my baby?" I cried. Tears streamed down my face, and I didn't know what to do or where to look for her.

Khol gripped my upper arms. "I want you to wait at the house. I'll search the area in a widening circle. Someone needs to stay here in case she returns." His intent gaze met mine. "I'm going to find her, Nancy. And I'm going to bring her back to you. She's safe." He pressed his fist against his chest. "I know this in my heart."

Would I be able to tell if she was hurt or . . . No, I wasn't going to think that. She was fine! We'd find her sitting under a tree, playing with one of her toys or reading a book.

In the rain?

I couldn't let myself believe we'd never find my daughter.

"I promise I'll bring her back safe," Khol said.

I nodded and while he rushed away, I slowly walked back to the house. Each of my footsteps made the dread build inside me.

And when I didn't find her waiting in the house, I only cried harder.

***

It seemed like forever passed before the doorknob rattled.

I burst up from the sofa and rushed over to it, flinging it wide.

Flora stood in the opening, her nightgown soaked, shivers wracking her tiny frame. She held a big pink shell in both hands.

"Sweetie," I cried, sweeping her up in my arms. "Where were you?" I peered outside, expecting to find Khol there, but we remained alone.

"I had-ta get Khol a pwesent," she exclaimed through her shivers. "A pwettty pink shell, Mommy."

"We don't leave the house without telling someone where we're going," I said. Fear kept bolting through me. She was back, but Khol wasn't.

I lowered her to the floor. "Wait here. Do not go outside!"

"Oh-kay," she said with the sigh of a put-upon teen.

I stepped outside, closing the door behind me, and started calling Khol's name.

He didn't reply, and he didn't come back.

I didn't dare venture far. I couldn't trust Flora not to follow. And she needed to get out of her wet things and into something dry.

He wasn't at the falls or anywhere near the meadow. The wind had died, thankfully, so I was sure my voice would carry as I shouted his name into the jungle.

"Where are you?" I whispered as I hurried back to the house.

Inside, I stripped off Flora's wet clothing and placed her in a warm tub, washing her quickly before drying her off and dressing her in the new nightie the house spirit provided.

I tucked her into bed, and I swore she was asleep before I reached her bedroom door, the pink shell she'd insisted on holding clutched in her arms like a stuffed bear.

I shut her door and peered around, hoping to find Khol waiting, but only silence greeted me.

And something odd.

A plate of cookies emerged from the counter. Sugar cookies—Khol's favorite kind. It was followed by a mug of the tea he preferred, plus a plate of vegetables and grains prepared exactly the way he liked them.

Looking at them only made me want to cry. Where was he?

I went outside, though again, I didn't dare venture far. I'd have stern words for Flora in the morning, though I'd focus more on her safety and not wanting to worry us. She needed to know she could never leave the house alone again.

Returning inside, I shut the door and sunk down on the couch that still held his scent.

It was a long night.

He hadn't returned by the time dawn cracked open the sky, heralding Christmas morning.

CHAPTER 28
KHOL

Flora was safe.

I'd searched the area surrounding my home in widening circles, finding no trace of the youngling. It was only when I was near the path leading to the ocean and about to turn around and return to our house, hoping to find her there, when I spied her tiny tracks leading to the sea.

Fear flashed through me as I raced in that direction. The storm had mostly passed, but the ocean would still be rough. Would Flora try to swim? The swift current would drag her away.

Racing from the jungle, I continued following her tracks all the way to where the waves crashed on the shore.

She wasn't there.

I kept picturing her in the water, fighting to stay close to shore while calling out for me and her mother.

That's when the water spirit spoke to me for the first time, though in my mind. The spirit didn't convey its message with words but with impressions. I saw Flora inside my house with Nancy, plus Nancy's fear when I didn't return. The spirit then suggested they would help me make Christmas the best holiday ever but that it would take time to do the preparations.

"I'll return and tell Nancy what I'm doing," I said, not wanting her to worry.

The water spirit told me they'd give Nancy signs to show her I was safe.

With my heart lighter, I returned to the jungle and took the trail toward the central hill, eager to follow the spirit's plan and return to Nancy and Flora by dawn.

CHAPTER 29
NANCY

Dawn split open the world, flooding Zuldrux with light. It found me where I sat on the sofa.

He hadn't come back, and I was desperate to run through the jungle, calling his name.

My chest ached and my throat hurt whenever I swallowed, but I hadn't gone to bed. As long as Khol was still out in the lingering storm, I'd wait for him.

"Where's Khol?" Flora asked, rushing out of her bedroom, dressed in a bright red onesie with green slippers courtesy of the house spirit. The outfit must've been waiting for her when she woke up. "And where's our stockings?" She peered around, her tiny face knit with concern.

I hadn't even noticed that the stockings were gone. Fear kept snarling through my heart, and it was all I could do to keep it from taking over.

"He'll be here soon." Please, be here soon.

Where was he and why hadn't he returned? He wouldn't leave us. I knew in my heart that Khol would always be here for me and my daughter.

Unless he physically couldn't reach us.

Flora had gotten up early. Somehow, kids always knew when it was Christmas. Every other day of the year, especially on the days when we had to get up early, I had to drag her from bed. But a day off and when Santa was coming?

"Do you want some breakfast?" I slid off the sofa and started toward the kitchen. I'd do normal things until he returned.

And he would return. I refused to believe anything else.

"Can we have waffles?" she chimed in, scooting to her chair. "Wit stwawberries and cweam?"

"Let's see what the water spirit has to say." Before I could formally ask, a plate holding something that looked like what she'd ordered appeared on the counter. I took it over to her along with the mug of tea gifted to me.

How could I drink or eat anything when Khol wasn't here with us?

Flora dug in, wiggling in her seat and humming Jingle Bells while she ate. She finished her meal, and I returned her plate to the counter. My tea remained untouched; I wouldn't be able to swallow.

"Where's Khol?" she asked again, hopping off her chair.

"He'll be here soon," I repeated by rote, hoping it would be true.

She spun in a circle, singing a song about Santa Clause coming to town. When she finished, she stood in front of the tree. "Look at all da pwesents! Can we open da pwesents, Mommy?"

"Once Khol gets here."

Her shoulders fell. "He needs to get here soon."

And that was when I heard the bells.

Flora paused and her head tilted, before she released a squeal and raced for the door. Wrenching it open, she burst into the sunshine, where she cried out with joy once again.

My heart leaping around behind my ribs, I hurried after her, stumbling over the jamb and out into the world washed new by the storm.

Santa had arrived—a blue-skinned Santa, that is.

He sat in a good approximation of a sleigh, dressed in a bright red suit with white trim and with our stuffed stockings lying on the bench beside him.

Eight creatures unlike any I'd seen before were harnessed to his wheeled sleigh, each sporting fake antlers strapped to their heads. Their brown fur fit with a reindeer, but their fangs and spiked tails gave the "eight tiny reindeer" idea a jarring feeling.

My laughter trilled, and I sobbed out my happiness that he was okay.

He climbed out of the sleigh, shouting. "Hay, hay, hay!"

"It's ho, ho, ho, Santa Khol," Flora said through her giggles. "*Ho*, not hay. We feed hay to da reindeer." Who she raced toward.

I grabbed her arm before she could reach them, holding her back. "Will they . . ."

"They're friendly—for now," he said, leaping from the sleigh. "As is this little one." He tugged a pink, fluffy creature the size of a kitten out of his pocket and held it out to Flora, who squealed.

"Kitty, kitty!" she said, hugging the tiny alien pet to her neck. "I's got a kitty. Thanks, Khol."

A pet. A new life. And the return of the male I was terrified I'd lose. Could life get better than this? It truly was a Christmas miracle.

While Flora took her new pet over to show the alien reindeer, he strode toward me like a god rising from the sea, all bold and gorgeous muscles rippling beneath his suit.

Even dressed in red and white, this guy was hot. I'd never get enough of him.

"I've been so worried about you," I said.

He paused in front of me, frowning. "The water spirit told me Flora came home. They said they told you I was okay."

"They didn't . . ." My heart lightened. "Ah. When your favorite cookies and meal appeared on the counter last night, I didn't know what to think."

"That was their sign. They told me about Flora in my mind."

If only they'd done the same for me. "It doesn't matter. You're safe. You're home."

His smile widened. "Yes, love, I'm home, with you and Flora. This is where I'll always belong."

He swept me up and kissed me.

And when he shouted ho, ho, ho, Flora and I joined in.

EPILOGUE
NANCY

Three Months Later

We spent the "winter" in our cozy home, and come spring, we took an everlipe, an enormous and surprisingly friendly stingray-like creature that skimmed across the water, to shore.

Three days of walking later—though Flora rode on her daddy's shoulders much of the way—we started up the path leading to the Indigan Clan. Our visit was a surprise, and I couldn't wait to see the other Earth women.

Depending on how things went there, he and I would talk about where we might live in the future. While we adored our island home, it was just us three. Khol and I didn't need anyone else, but Flora needed friends and socialization with younglings her own age. We'd talked about moving to one of the sky islands and in with the Dastalon Clan, but Khol still wanted to put his past behind him. Possibly moving in with the Indigan Clan would still give him the fresh start he craved but would fit our other needs.

If things worked out, we'd build a permanent home here and travel to our cozy island a few times a year for vacation.

The best thing of all was that the water spirit—with my help—crafted a message to send to my mom, telling her Flora and I were safe and explaining about the kidnapping and being brought here. The water spirit even sent us her reply. She'd miss us, but knowing we were safe and loved was all that mattered.

Maybe someday, I'd see her again.

We reached the outskirts of the Indigan Clan, though Khol didn't need to tell me.

The smell of real pizza did it for me.

My grin rose, so big it made my face ache.

"Pizza," Flora cried, dancing in a circle on Khol's shoulders, her new pet "kitty," Flower, on her shoulder. "I want pizza! Pepperoni."

She'd made amazing strides with her home speech therapy.

"So do I, sweetie," I said ruefully. "So do I." Pizza was one of the few meals the water spirit couldn't quite get right. Maybe it was their cheese that held a rubbery texture. Or their purple tomato sauce that didn't taste like tomatoes. Or their pepperoni that might look vaguely like what I remembered from Earth but melted when you placed it in your mouth.

A sound in the woods behind us sent me spinning. At first, I thought it must be a drettire, the purple, squirrel-like creatures Flora sometimes called kitties.

But then I saw him. Khol was a big guy, especially when compared to a human male, but this guy . . . He had to be at least five inches taller than Khol, and he was wider.

My gaze met his, and I saw so much sadness there, that I couldn't suck in a breath. Such profound loneliness. My bones ached in sympathy. Was he one of the Indigan Clan?

Khol stopped beside me, and I turned to face him. "What's wrong?" he asked.

"It's—" When I looked toward the woods again, the male was gone. Had I truly seen him or was the sunlight streaking through the thick lavender vegetation playing tricks on my eyes?

The more I stared in that direction, not seeing anything, the more doubts crowded into my mind.

"Nothing," I finally said, and we continued walking.

We climbed the hill and rounded a bend. I gasped, coming to a stop, gazing at enormous, blue-scaled creatures that glimmered in the sunlight as if they were made of crystal. But they couldn't be, could they?

"Hepadons," Khol said with a smile. "If we live here, we'll raise a few to ride."

"How do you get up on something the size of a minivan?"

"You'll see." He was used to me using Earth terms as comparison, and he'd heard of minivans already.

"Oh, my god," someone cried out from farther up the hill.

Three women raced toward us with their hair flying out behind them, followed sedately by Zuldruxian males.

"Go," Khol said with a smile, urging me to meet them.

"I wanna run too," Flora said with a pout.

He lowered her to the ground, and I took her hand.

Laughing, we raced toward the women, and when we reached them, we all stopped, staring at each other in awe.

"I'm Vanessa," one said. She glanced over her shoulder. "My gorgeous mate is Aizor."

One of the males stopped behind her and grunted, his gaze scanning my frame in a polite way. His arm went around Vanessa's waist, and when the fabric pressed close, it outlined the start of a baby belly. Pregnant?

I suspected I might be as well.

Tears filled my eyes at the thought of having friends, of seeing my children growing up in this amazing world with others just like them.

"I'm Nancy," I said, wiping away my tears.

One of the other women barreled into me, lifting me off my feet for a hug. "I'm Amanda. I'm with the gruff guy, Xax." She lowered me to my feet but kept hold of my hands. "And this," she tilted her head toward the third woman, "is Kerry. She and Nevarn have mated as well. Welcome."

"Welcome," Kerry echoed with a big smile. Nevarn nodded.

I took in the males standing nearby, their protective gazes on their women, and my heart soared.

And while Flora danced around us all, showing off Flower to her new friends, Khol came up behind me and placed his hands on my shoulders. Leaning forward, he kissed my cheek.

"Happy, mate?" he whispered by my ear.

"Yes," I said, my face stretching in an even bigger grin. As wonderful as it was to meet new people, I was already secure and content with my mate.

Tipping my head back, I smiled up at him. "I couldn't be happier."

I hope you enjoyed Nancy & Khol's holiday story!

Pick up the rest of the Zuldrux Warriors Series here.

About the Author

Ava Ross is a two-time *USA Today* Bestselling author who has written numerous titles, all of them featuring sweet and steamy romance. She fell for men with unusual features when she first watched Star Wars, where alien creatures have gone mainstream. She lives in New England with her husband (who is sadly not an alien, though he is still cute in his own way), her kids, and a few assorted pets.

ALSO BY AVA ROSS

You can find Ava's books on <u>Amazon</u> & on her website at avarosswrites(dot)com.